I0661045

Octave Thanet

Stories of a western town

Octave Thanet

Stories of a western town

ISBN/EAN: 9783743302983

Manufactured in Europe, USA, Canada, Australia, Japa

Cover: Foto ©ninafisch / pixelio.de

Manufactured and distributed by brebook publishing software
(www.brebook.com)

Octave Thanet

Stories of a western town

It was Tommy Fitzmaurice, grown into a handsome young man.

STORIES OF

A WESTERN TOWN

BY

OCTAVE THANET

ILLUSTRATED BY A. B. FROST

NEW YORK
CHARLES SCRIBNER'S SONS
1893

Press of J. J. Little & Co.
Astor Place, New York

CONTENTS

LIST OF ILLUSTRATIONS

STORIES OF
A WESTERN TOWN

"No, it was not fair to thee— I know that now"

THE BESETMENT OF
KURT LIEDERS

A SILVER rime glistened all down the street.
There was a drabble of dead leaves on the
sidewalk which was of wood, and on the roadway
which was of macadam and stiff mud. The wind
blew sharply, for it was a December day and only
six in the morning. Nor were the houses high
enough to furnish any independent bulwark;
they were low, wooden dwellings, the tallest a
bare two stories in height, the majority only one
story. But they were in good painting and
repair, and most of them had a homely gayety of
geraniums or bouvardias in the windows. The
house on the corner was the tall house. It occupied a larger yard than its neighbors; and there
were lace curtains tied with blue ribbons for the
windows in the right hand front room. The door
of this house swung back with a crash, and a
woman darted out. She ran at the top of her
speed to the little yellow house farther down the

street. Her blue calico gown clung about her stout figure and fluttered behind her, revealing her blue woollen stockings and felt slippers. Her gray head was bare. As she ran tears rolled down her cheeks and she wrung her hands.

"Oh! Oh! Oh! Oh, lieber Herr Je!" One near would have heard her sob, in too distracted agitation to heed the motorneer of the passing street-car who stared after her at the risk of his car, or the tousled heads behind a few curtains. She did not stop until she almost fell against the door of the yellow house. Her frantic knocking was answered by a young woman in a light and artless costume of a quilted petticoat and a red flannel sack.

"Oh, gracious goodness! Mrs. Lieders!" cried she.

Thekla Lieders rather staggered than walked into the room and fell back on the black haircloth sofa.

"There, there, there," said the young woman while she patted the broad shoulders heaving between sobs and short breath, "what is it? The house aint afire?"

"Oh, no, oh, Mrs. Olsen, he has done it again!" She wailed in sobs, like a child.

"Done it? Done what?" exclaimed Mrs.

Olsen, then her face paled. "Oh, my gracious, you *don't* mean he's killed himself——"

"Yes, he's killed himself, again."

"And he's dead?" asked the other in an awed tone.

Mrs. Lieders gulped down her tears. "Oh, not so bad as that, I cut him down, he was up in the garret and I sus—suspected him and I run up and—oh, he was there, a choking, and he was so mad! He swore at me and—he kicked me when I—I says: 'Kurt, what are you doing of? Hold on till I git a knife,' I says—for his hands was just dangling at his side; and he says nottings cause he couldn't, he · was most gone, and I knowed I wouldn't have time to git no knife but I saw it was a rope was pretty bad worn and so— so I just run and jumped and ketched it in my hands, and being I'm so fleshy it couldn't stand no more and it broke! And, oh! he—he kicked me when I was try to come near to git the rope off his neck; and so soon like he could git his breath he swore at me——"

"And you a helping of him! Just listen to that!" cried the hearer indignantly.

"So I come here for to git you and Mr. Olsen to help me git him down stairs, 'cause he is too heavy for me to lift, and he is so mad he won't walk down himself."

" He swore at me."

"Yes, yes, of course. I'll call Carl. Carl! dost thou hear? come! But did you dare to leave him, Mrs. Lieders?" Part of the time she spoke in English, part of the time in her own tongue, gliding from one to another, and neither party observing the transition.

Mrs. Lieders wiped her eyes, saying: "Oh, yes, Danke schön, I aint afraid 'cause I tied him with the rope, righd good, so he don't got no chance to move. He was make faces at me all the time I tied him." At the remembrance, the tears welled anew.

Mrs. Olsen, a little bright tinted woman with a nose too small for her big blue eyes and chubby cheeks, quivered with indignant sympathy.

"Well, I did nefer hear of sooch a mean acting man!" seemed to her the most natural expression; but the wife fired, at once.

"No, he is not a mean man," she cried, "no, Freda Olsen, he is not a mean man at all! There aint nowhere a better man than my man; and Carl Olsen, he knows that. Kurt, he always buys a whole ham and a whole barrel of flour, and never less than a dollar of sugar at a time! And he never gits drunk nor he never gives me any bad talk. It was only he got this wanting to kill himself on him, sometimes."

"Well, I guess I'll go put on my things," said Mrs. Olsen, wisely declining to defend her position. "You set right still and warm yourself, and we'll be back in a minute."

Indeed, it was hardly more than that time before both Carl Olsen, who worked in the same furniture factory as Kurt Lieders, and was a comely and after-witted giant, appeared with Mrs. Olsen ready for the street.

He nodded at Mrs. Lieders and made a gurgling noise in his throat, expected to convey sympathy. Then, he coughed and said that he was ready, and they started.

Feeling further expression demanded, Mrs. Olsen asked: "How many times has he done it, Mrs. Lieders?"

Mrs. Lieders was trotting along, her anxious eyes on the house in the distance, especially on the garret windows. "Three times," she answered, not removing her eyes; "onct he tooked Rough on Rats and I found it out and I put some apple butter in the place of it, and he kept wondering and wondering how he didn't feel notings, and after awhile I got him off the notion, that time. He wasn't mad at me; he just said: 'Well, I do it some other time. You see!' but he promised to wait till I got the spring house cleaning over, so he could shake the carpets for me; and by and by he got feeling better. He was mad at the boss and that made him feel bad. The next time it was the same, that time he jumped into the cistern——"

"Yes, I know," said Olsen, with a half grin, "I pulled him out."

"It was the razor he wanted," the wife continued, "and when he come home and says he was going to leave the shop and he aint never going back there, and gets out his razor and sharps it, I knowed what that meant and I told him I got to have some bluing and wouldn't he go and get it? and he says, 'You won't git another husband run so free on your errands, Thekla,' and I says I don't want none; and when he was gone I hid the razor and he couldn't find it, but that didn't mad him, he didn't say notings; and when I went to git the supper he walked out in the yard and jumped into the cistern, and I heard the splash and looked in and there he was trying to git his head under, and I called, 'For the Lord's sake, papa! For the Lord's sake!' just like that. And I fished for him with the pole that stood there and he was sorry and caught hold of it and give in, and I rested the pole agin the side cause I wasn't

strong enough to h'ist him out ; and he held on
whilest I run for help——"

"And I got the ladder and he clum out," said
the giant with another grin of recollection, " he
was awful wet !"

"That was a month ago," said the wife, solemnly.

" He sharped the razor onct," said Mrs. Lieders, " but he said it was for to shave him, and I
got him to promise to let the barber shave him
sometime, instead. Here, Mrs. Olsen, you go
righd in, the door aint locked."

By this time they were at the house door.
They passed in and ascended the stairs to the
second story, then climbed a narrow, ladder-like
flight to the garret. Involuntarily they had
paused to listen at the foot of the stairs, but it
was very quiet, not a sound of movement, not so
much as the sigh of a man breathing. The wife
turned pale and put both her shaking hands on
her heart.

"Guess he's trying to scare us by keeping
quiet!" said Olsen, cheerfully, and he stumbled
up the stairs, in advance. " Thunder!" he exclaimed, on the last stair, " well, we aint any too
quick."

In fact Carl had nearly fallen over the master of the house, that enterprising self-destroyer having contrived, pinioned as he was, to roll over to the very brink of the stair well, with the plain intent to break his neck by plunging headlong.

In the dim light all that they could see was a small, old man whose white hair was strung in wisps over his purple face, whose deep set eyes glared like the eyes of a rat in a trap, and whose very elbows and knees expressed in their cramps the fury of an outraged soul. When he saw the new-comers he shut his eyes and his jaws.

"Well, Mr. Lieders," said Olsen, mildly, "I guess you better git down-stairs. Kin I help you up?"

"No," said Lieders.

"Will I give you an arm to lean on?"

"No."

"Won't you go at all, Mr. Lieders?"

"No."

Olsen shook his head. "I hate to trouble you, Mr. Lieders," said he in his slow, undecided tones, "please excuse me," with which he gathered up the little man into his strong arms and slung him over his shoulders, as easily as

he would sling a sack of meal. It was a vent
for Mrs. Olsen's bubbling indignation to make
a dive for Lieders's heels and hold them, while
Carl backed down-stairs. But Lieders did not
make the least resistance. He allowed them to
carry him into the room indicated by his wife,
and to lay him bound on the plump feather
bed. It was not his bedroom but the sacred
"spare room," and the bed was part of its
luxury. Thekla ran in, first, to remove the
embroidered pillow shams and the dazzling,
silken "crazy quilt" that was her choicest pos-
session.

Safely in the bed, Lieders opened his eyes
and looked from one face to the other, his lip
curling. "You can't keep me this way all the
time. I can do it in spite of you," said he.

"Well, I think you had ought to be ashamed
of yourself, Mr. Lieders!" Mrs. Olsen burst out,
in a tremble between wrath and exertion, shaking
her little, plump fist at him.

But the placid Carl only nodded, as in sympathy, saying, "Well, I am sorry you feel so bad,
Mr. Lieders. I guess we got to go now."

Mrs. Olsen looked as if she would have liked
to exhort Lieders further; but she shrugged

her shoulders and followed her husband in silence.

"I wished you'd stay to breakfast, now you're here," Thekla urged out of her imperious hospitality; had Kurt been lying there dead, the next meal must have been offered, just the same. "I know, you aint got time to git Mr. Olsen his breakfast, Freda, before he has got to go to the shops, and my tea-kettle is boiling now, and the coffee'll be ready—I *guess* you had better stay."

But Mrs. Olsen seconded her husband's denial, and there was nothing left Thekla but to see them to the door. No sooner did she return than Lieders spoke. "Aint you going to take off them ropes?" said he.

"Not till you promise you won't do it."

Silence. Thekla, brushing a few tears from her eyes, scrutinized the ropes again, before she walked heavily out of the room. She turned the key in the door.

Directly a savory steam floated through the hall and pierced the cracks about the door; then Thekla's footsteps returned; they echoed over the uncarpeted boards.

She had brought his breakfast, cooked with the best of her homely skill. The pork chops that he

liked had been fried, there was a napkin on the
tray, and the coffee was in the best gilt cup and
saucer.

"Here's your breakfast, papa," said she, trying
to smile.

"I don't want no breakfast," said he.

She waited, holding the tray, and wistfully ey-
ing him.

"Take it 'way," said he, "I won't touch it if
you stand till doomsday, lessen you untie me!"

"I'll untie your arm, papa, one arm; you
kin eat that way."

"Not lessen you untie all of me, I won't
touch a bite."

"You know why I won't untie you, papa."

"Starving will kill as dead as hanging," was
Lieders's orphic response to this.

Thekla sighed and went away, leaving the
tray on the table. It may be that she hoped
the sight of food might stir his stomach to
rebel against his dogged will; if so she was
disappointed; half an hour went by during
which the statue under the bedclothes remained
without so much as a quiver.

Then the old woman returned. "Aint you
awful cramped and stiff, papa?"

" Yes," said the statue.

" Will you promise not to do yourself a mischief, if I untie you ? "

" No."

Thekla groaned, while the tears started to her red eyelids. " But you'll git awful tired and it will hurt you if you don't get the ropes off, soon, papa ! "

" I know that ! "

He closed his eyes again, to be the less hindered from dropping back into his distempered musings. Thekla took a seat by his side and sat silent as he. Slowly the natural pallor returned to the high forehead and sharp features. They were delicate features and there was an air of refinement, of thought, about Lieders's whole person, as different as possible from the robust comeliness of his wife. With its keen sensitiveness and its undefined melancholy it was a dreamer's face. One meets such faces, sometimes, in incongruous places and wonders what they mean. In fact, Kurt Lieders, head cabinet maker in the furniture factory of Lossing & Co., was an artist. He was, also, an incomparable artisan and the most exacting foreman in the shops. Thirty years ago he had first taken wages

from the senior Lossing. He had watched a
modest industry climb up to a great business, nor
was he all at sea in his own estimate of his share
in the firm's success. Lieders's workmanship had
an honesty, an infinite patience of detail, a daring
skill of design that came to be sought and commanded its own price. The Lossing " art furniture " did not slander the name. No sculptor
ever wrought his soul into marble with a more
unflinching conscience or a purer joy in his
work than this wood-carver dreaming over sideboards and bedsteads. Unluckily, Lieders had
the wrong side of the gift as well as the right ;
was full of whims and crotchets, and as unpracti-
cal as the Christian martyrs. He openly defied
expense, and he would have no trifling with
the laws of art. To make after orders was an
insult to Kurt. He made what was best for
the customer ; if the latter had not the sense
to see it he was a fool and a pig, and some one
else should work for him, not Kurt Lieders,
begehr !

Young Lossing had learned the business practi-
cally. He was taught the details by his father's
best workman ; and a mighty hard and strict
master the best workman proved↓ Lossing did

not dream that the crabbed old tyrant who rarely
praised him, who made him go over, for the
twentieth time, any imperfect piece of work, who
exacted all the artisan virtues to the last inch,
was secretly proud of him. Yet, in fact, the
thread of romance in Lieders's prosaic life was his
idolatry of the Lossing Manufacturing Co. It is
hard to tell whether it was the Lossings or that
intangible quantity, the firm, the business, that he
worshipped. Worship he did, however, the one
or the other, perhaps the both of them, though in
the peevish and erratic manner of the savage who
sometimes grovels to his idols and sometimes
kicks them.

Nobody guessed what a blow it was to Kurt
when, a year ago, the elder Lossing had died.
Even his wife did not connect his sullen melancholy and his gibes at the younger generation,
with the crape on Harry Lossing's hat. He
would not go to the funeral, but worked savagely,
all alone by himself, in the shop, the whole afternoon—breaking down at last at the sight of a
carved panel over which Lossing and he had once
disputed. The desolate loneliness of the old
came to him when his old master was gone. He
loved the young man, but the old man was of

2

his own generation ; he had " known how things
ought to be and he could understand without
talking." Lieders began to be on the lookout for
signs of waning consideration, to watch his own
eyes and hands, drearily wondering when they
would begin to play him false ; at the same time
because he was unhappy he was ten times as
exacting and peremptory and critical with the
younger workmen, and ten times as insolently
independent with the young master. Often
enough, Lossing was exasperated to the point of
taking the old man at his word and telling him to
go if he would, but every time the chain of long
habit, a real respect for such faithful service, and
a keen admiration for Kurt's matchless skill in his
craft, had held him back. He prided himself on
keeping his word ; for that reason he was warier
of using it. So he would compromise by giving
the domineering old fellow a "good, stiff rowing."
Once, he coupled this with a threat, if they could
not get along decently they would better part !
Lieders had answered not a word ; he had given
Lossing a queer glance and turned on his heel.
He went home and bought some poison on the
way. " The old man is gone and the young feller
don't want the old crank round, no more," he

said to himself. "Thekla, I guess I make her troubles, too ; I'll git out !"

That was the beginning of his tampering with suicide. Thekla, who did not have the same opinion of the "trouble," had interfered. He had married Thekla to have someone to keep a warm fireside for him, but she was an ignorant creature who never could be made to understand about carving. He felt sorry for her when the baby died, the only child they ever had ; he was sorrier than he expected to be on his own account, too, for it was an ugly little creature, only four days old, and very red and wrinkled ; but he never thought of confiding his own griefs or trials to her. Now, it made him angry to have that stupid Thekla keep him in a world where he did not wish to stay. If the next day Lossing had not remembered how his father valued Lieders, and made an excuse to half apologize to him, I fear Thekla's stratagems would have done little good.

The next experience was cut out of the same piece of cloth. He had relented, he had allowed his wife to save him ; but he was angry in secret. Then came the day when open disobedience to Lossing's orders had snapped the last thread of

Harry's patience. To Lieders's aggrieved "If you ain't satisfied with my work, Mr. Lossing, I kin quit," the answer had come instantly, "Very well, Lieders, I'm sorry to lose you, but we can't have two bosses here: you can go to the desk." And when Lieders in a blind stab of temper had growled a prophecy that Lossing would regret it, Lossing had stabbed in turn: "Maybe, but it will be a cold day when I ask you to come back." And he had gone off without so much as a word of regret. The old workman had packed up his tools, the pet tools that no one was ever permitted to touch, and crammed his arms into his coat and walked out of the place where he had worked so long, not a man saying a word. Lieders didn't reflect that they knew nothing of the quarrel. He glowered at them and went away sore at heart. We make a great mistake when we suppose that it is only the affectionate that desire affection; sulky and ill-conditioned souls often have a passionate longing for the very feelings that they repel. Lieders was a womanish, sensitive creature under the surly mask, and he was cut to the quick by his comrades' apathy. "There ain't no place for old men in this world," he thought, "there's them boys I done my best to make do a good job, and some of 'em I've worked overtime to help ; and not one of 'em has got as much as a good-by in him for me ! "

But he did not think of going to poor Thekla for comfort, he went to his grim dreams. " I git my property all straight for Thekla, and then I quit," said he. Perhaps he gave himself a reprieve unconsciously, thinking that something might happen to save him from himself. Nothing happened. None of the "boys" came to see him, except Carl Olsen, the very stupidest man in the shop, who put Lieders beside himself fifty times a day. The other men were sorry that Lieders had gone, having a genuine workman's admiration for his skill, and a sort of underground liking for the unreasonable old man because he was so absolutely honest and "a fellow could always tell where to find him." But they were shy, they were afraid he would take their pity in bad part, they "waited a while."

Carl, honest soul, stood about in Lieders's workshop, kicking the shavings with his heels for half an hour, and grinned sheepishly, and was told what a worthless, scamping, bragging lot the "boys" at Lossing's were, and said he guessed he had got to go home now ; and so departed, un-

witting that his presence had been a consola-
tion. Mrs. Olsen asked Carl what Lieders said;

None of the "boys" came to see him, except Carl Olsen.

Carl answered simply, "Say, Freda, that man
feels terrible bad."

Meanwhile Thekla seemed easily satisfied. She

made no outcry as Lieders had dreaded, over his
leaving the shop.

" Well, then, papa, you don't need git up so
early in the morning no more, if you aint going to the shop," was her only comment; and
Lieders despised the mind of woman more than
ever.

But that evening, while Lieders was down town
(occupied, had she known it, with a codicil to his
will), she went over to the Olsens and found out
all Carl could tell her about the trouble in the
shop.   And it was she that made the excuse of
marketing to go out the next day, that she might
see the rich widow on the hill who was talking
about a china closet, and Judge Trevor, who had
asked the price of a mantel, and Mr. Martin, who
had looked at sideboards (all this information
came from honest Carl); and who proposed to
them that they order such furniture of the best
cabinet-maker in the country, now setting up on
his own account.   He, simple as a baby for all his
doggedness, thought that they came because of
his fame as a workman, and felt a glow of pride,
particularly as (having been prepared by the wife,
who said, " You see it don't make so much differ-
ence with my Kurt 'bout de prize, if so he can

get the furniture like he wants it, and he always
know of the best in the old country") they all
were duly humble. He accepted a few orders
and went to work with a will; he would show
them what the old man could do. But it was
only a temporary gleam; in a little while he grew
homesick for the shop, for the sawdust floor and
the familiar smell of oil, and the picture of Lossing flitting in and out. He missed the careless
young workmen at whom he had grumbled, he
missed the whir of machinery, and the conscious-
ness of rush and hurry accented by the cars on
the track outside. In short, he missed the feeling of being part of a great whole. At home, in
his cosey little improvised shop, there was none
to dispute him, but there was none to obey him
either. He grew deathly tired of it all. He got
into the habit of walking around the shops at
night, prowling about his old haunts like a cat.
Once the night watchman saw him. The next
day there was a second watchman engaged. And
Olsen told him very kindly, meaning only to warn
him, that he was suspected to be there for no
good purpose. Lieders confirmed a lurking suspicion of the good Carl's own, by the clouding
of his face. Yet he would have chopped his

hand off rather than have lifted it against the shop.

That was Tuesday night, this was Wednesday morning.

The memory of it all, the cruel sense of injustice, returned with such poignant force that Lieders groaned aloud.

Instantly, Thekla was bending over him. He did not know whether to laugh at her or to swear, for she began fumbling at the ropes, half sobbing. "Yes, I knowed they was hurting you, papa; I'm going to loose one arm. Then I put it back again and loose the other. Please don't be bad!"

He made no resistance and she was as good as her word. She unbound and bound him in sections, as it were; he watching her with a morose smile.

Then she left the room, but only to return with some hot coffee. Lieders twisted his head away. "No," said he, "I don't eat none of that breakfast, not if you make fresh coffee all the morning; I feel like I don't eat never no more on earth."

Thekla knew that the obstinate nature that she tempted was proof against temptation; if

Kurt chose to starve, starve he would with food at his elbow.

"Oh, papa," she cried, helplessly, "what *is* the matter with you?"

"Just dying is the matter with me, Thekla. If I can't die one way I kin another. Now Thekla, I want you to quit crying and listen. After I'm gone you go to the boss, young Mr. Lossing—but I always called him Harry because he learned his trade of me, Thekla, but he don't think of that now—and you tell him old Lieders that worked for him thirty years is dead, but he didn't hold no hard feelings, he knowed he done wrong 'bout that mantel. Mind you tell him."

"Yes, papa," said Thekla, which was a surprise to Kurt; he had dreaded a weak flood of tears and protestations. But there were no tears, no protestations, only a long look at him and a contraction of the eyebrows as if Thekla were trying to think of something that eluded her. She placed the coffee on the tray beside the other breakfast. For a while the room was very still. Lieders could not see the look of resolve that finally smoothed the perplexed lines out of his wife's kind, simple old face.

She rose. "Kurt," she said, "I don't guess you remember this is our wedding-day; it was this day, eighteen year we was married."

"So!" said Lieders, "well, I was a bad bargain to you, Thekla; after you nursed your father that was a cripple for twenty years, I thought it would be easy with me; but I was a bad bargain."

"The Lord knows best about that," said Thekla, simply, "be it how it be, you are the only man I ever had or will have, and I don't like you starve yourself. Papa, say you don't kill yourself, to-day, and dat you will eat your breakfast!"

"Yes," Lieders repeated in German, "a bad bargain for thee, that is sure. But thou hast been a good bargain for me. Here! I promise. Not this day. Give me the coffee."

He had seasons, all the morning, of wondering over his meekness, and his agreement to be tied up again, at night. But still, what did a day matter? a man humors women's notions; and starving was so tedious. Between whiles he elaborated a scheme to attain his end. How easy to outwit the silly Thekla! His eyes shone, as he hid the little, sharp knife up his cuff.

"Let her tie me!" says Lieders, "I keep my word. To-morrow I be out of this. He won't git a man like me, pretty soon!"

Thekla went about her daily tasks, with her every-day air; but, now and again, that same pucker of thought returned to her forehead; and, more than once, Lieders saw her stand over some dish, poising her spoon in air, too abstracted to notice his cynical observation.

The dinner was more elaborate than common, and Thekla had broached a bottle of her currant wine. She gravely drank Lieders's health. "And many good days, papa," she said.

Lieders felt a queer move-

"He wiped dishes as he did everything, neatly slowly."

ment of pity. After the table was cleared, he
helped his wife to wash and wipe the dishes as
his custom was of a Sunday or holiday. He
wiped dishes as he did everything, neatly, slowly,
with a careful deliberation. Not until the dishes
were put away and the couple were seated, did
Thekla speak.

" Kurt," she said, " I got to talk to you."

An inarticulate groan and a glance at the door
from Lieders. " I just got to, papa. It aint
righd for you to do the way you been doing for
so long time ; efery little whiles you try to kill
yourself ; no, papa, that aint righd ! "

Kurt, who had gotten out his pencils and com-
passes and other drawing tools, grunted : " I got
to look at my work, Thekla, now ; I am too busy
to talk."

" No, Kurt, no, papa "—the hands holding the
blue apron that she was embroidering with white
linen began to tremble ; Lieders had not the least
idea what a strain it was on this reticent, slow of
speech woman who had stood in awe of him for
eighteen years, to discuss the horror of her life ;
but he could not help marking her agitation.
She went on, desperately : " Yes, papa, I got to
talk it oud with you. You had ought to listen,

'cause I always been a good wife to you and nefer refused you notings. No."

" Well, I aint saying I done it 'cause *you* been bad to me ; everybody knows we aint had no trouble."

" But everybody what don't know us, when they read how you tried to kill yourself in the papers, they think it was me. That always is so. And now I never can any more sleep nights, for you is always maybe git up and do something to yourself. So now, I got to talk to you, papa. Papa, how could you done so ?"

Lieders twisted his feet under the rungs of his chair; he opened his mouth, but only to shut it again with a click of his teeth.

" I got my mind made up, papa. I tought and I tought. I know *why* you done it ; you done it 'cause you and the boss was mad at each other. The boss hadn't no righd to let you go——"

" Yes, he had, I madded him first ; I was a fool. Of course I knowed more than him 'bout the work, but I hadn't no right to go against him. The boss is all right."

" Yes, papa, I got my mind made up"—like most sluggish spirits there was an immense

momentum about Thekla's mind, once get it
fairly started it was not to be diverted—" you
never killed yourself before you used to git mad
at the boss. You was afraid he would send you
away; and now you have sent yourself away you
don't want to live, 'cause you do not know how
you can git along without the shop. But you
want to get back, you want to get back more as
you want to kill yourself. Yes, papa, I know, I
know where you did used to go, nights. Now"
—she changed her speech unconsciously to the
tongue of her youth—" it is not fair, it is not fair
to me that thou shouldst treat me like that, thou
dost belong to me, also ; so I say, my Kurt, wilt
thou make a bargain with me? If I shall get
thee back thy place wilt thou promise me never
to kill thyself any more?"

Lieders had not once looked up at her during
the slow, difficult sentences with their half
choked articulation; but he was experiencing
some strange emotions, and one of them was a
novel respect for his wife. All he said was :
" 'Taint no use talking. I won't never ask him
to take me back, once."

"Well, you aint asking of him. *I* ask him. I
try to git you back, once!"

" I tell you, it aint no use; I know the boss, he
aint going to be letting womans talk him over;
no, he's a good man, he knows how to work his
business himself!"

" But would you promise me, Kurt?"

Lieders's eyes blurred with a mild and dreamy
mist; he sighed softly. " Thekla, you can't see
how it is. It is like you are tied up, if I don't
can do that; if I can then it is always that I am
free, free to go, free to stay. And for you,
Thekla, it is the same."

Thekla's mild eyes flashed. " I don't believe
you would like it so you wake up in the morning
and find *me* hanging up in the kitchen by the
clothes-line!"

Lieders had the air of one considering deeply.
Then he gave Thekla one of the surprises of her
life; he rose from his chair, he walked in his shuf-
fling, unheeled slippers across the room to where
the old woman sat; he put one arm on the back
of the chair and stiffly bent over her and kissed
her.

" Lieber Herr Je!" gasped Thekla.

" Then I shall go, too, pretty quick, that is all,
mamma," said he.

Thekla wiped her eyes. A little pause fell

3

between them, and in it they may have both
remembered vanished, half-forgotten days when
life had looked differently to them, when they
had never thought to sit by their own fireside
and discuss suicide. The husband spoke first;
with a reluctant, half-shamed smile, " Thekla, I
tell you what, I make the bargain with you;
you git me back that place, I don't do it again,
'less you let me; you don't git me back that
place, you don't say notings to me."

The apron dropped from the withered, brown
hands to the floor. Again there was silence; but
not for long; ghastly as was the alternative, the
proposal offered a chance to escape from the
terror that was sapping her heart.

" How long will you give me, papa ?" said she.

" I give you a week," said he.

Thekla rose and went to the door; as she
opened it a fierce gust of wind slashed her like
a knife, and Lieders exclaimed, fretfully, " what
you opening that door for, Thekla, letting in the
wind ? I'm so cold, now, right by the fire, I
most can't draw. We got to keep a fire in the
base-burner good, all night, or the plants will
freeze."

Thekla said confusedly that something sounded

like a cat crying. "And you talking like that it frightened me ; maybe I was wrong to make such bargains——"

"Then don't make it," said Lieders, curtly, " I aint asking you."

But Thekla drew a long breath and straightened herself, saying, "Yes, I make it, papa, I make it."

" Well, put another stick of wood in the stove, will you, now you are up?" said Lieders, shrugging his shoulders, "or I'll freeze in spite of you ! It seems to me it grows colder every minute."

But all that day he was unusually gentle with Thekla. He talked of his youth and the struggles of the early days of the firm ; he related a dozen tales of young Lossing, all illustrating some admirable trait that he certainly had not praised at the time. Never had he so opened his heart in regard to his own ideals of art, his own ambitions. And Thekla listened, not always comprehending but always sympathizing ; she was almost like a comrade, Kurt thought afterward.

The next morning, he was surprised to have her appear equipped for the street, although it was bitterly cold. She wore her garb of ceremony, a black alpaca gown, with a white crocheted collar

neatly turned over the long black, broadcloth
cloak in which she had taken pride for the last
five years ; and her quilted black silk bonnet was
on her gray head. When she put up her foot to
don her warm overshoes Kurt saw that the stout
ankles were encased in white stockings. This
was the last touch. " Gracious, Thekla," cried
Kurt, " are you going to market this day ? It is
the coldest day this winter ! "

" Oh, I don't mind," replied Thekla, nervously.
Then she had wrapped a scarf about her and
gone out while he was getting into his own coat,
and conning a proffer to go in her stead.

" Oh, well, Thekla she aint such a fool like she
looks ! " he observed to the cat, " say, pussy, *was*
it you out yestiddy ? "

The cat only blinked her yellow eyes and
purred. She knew that she had not been out,
last night. Not any better than her mistress,
however, who at this moment was hailing a
street-car.

The street-car did not land her anywhere near
a market ; it whirled her past the lines of low
wooden houses into the big brick shops with
their arched windows and terra-cotta ornaments
that showed the ambitious architecture of a

growing Western town, past these into mills and factories and smoke-stained chimneys. Here, she stopped. An acquaintance would hardly have recognized her, her ruddy cheeks had grown so pale. But she trotted on to the great building on the corner from whence came a low, incessant buzz. She went into the first door and ran against Carl Olsen. "Carl, I got to see Mr. Lossing," said she breathlessly.

"There ain't noding——"

"No, Gott sei dank', but I got to see him."

It was not Carl's way to ask questions; he promptly showed her the office and she entered. She had not seen young Harry Lossing half a dozen times; and, now, her anxious eyes wandered from one dapper figure at the high desks, to another, until Lossing advanced to her.

He was a handsome young man, she thought, and he had kind eyes, but they hardened at her first timid sentence: "I am Mrs. Lieders, I come about my man——"

"Will you walk in here, Mrs. Lieders?" said Lossing. His voice was like the ice on the window-panes.

She followed him into a little room. He shut the door.

Declining the chair that he pushed toward her
she stood in the centre of the room, looking at
him with the pleading eyes of a child.

"Mr. Lossing, will you please save my Kurt
from killing himself?"

"What do you mean?" Lossing's voice had
not thawed.

"It is for you that he will kill himself, Mr.
Lossing. This is the dird time he has done it.
It is because he is so lonesome now, your father
is died and he thinks that you forget, and he has
worked so hard for you, but he thinks that you
forget. He was never tell me till yesterday; and
then—it was—it was because I would not let him
hang himself———"

"Hang himself?" stammered Lossing, "you
don't mean——"

"Yes, he was hang himself, but I cut him, no I
broke him down," said Thekla, accurate in all the
disorder of her spirits; and forthwith, with many
tremors, but clearly, she told the story of Kurt's
despair. She told, as Lieders never would have
known how to tell, even had his pride let him, all
the man's devotion for the business, all his per-
sonal attachment to the firm; she told of his
gloom after the elder Lossing died, "for he was

think there was no one in this town such good
man and so smart like your fader, Mr. Lossing,
no, and he would set all the evening and try

" Hang himself ? " stammered Lossing.

to draw and make the lines all wrong, and, then,
he would drow the papers in the fire and go
and walk outside and he say, 'I can't do nothing
righd no more now the old man's died; they don't
have no use for me at the shop, pretty quick!' and

that make him feel awful bad!" She told of his
homesick wanderings about the shops by night;
"but he was better as a watchman, he wouldn't
hurt it for the world! He telled me how you
was hide his dinner-pail onct for a joke, and put
in a piece of your pie, and how you climbed on
the roof with the hose when it was afire. And
he telled me if he shall die I shall tell you that
he ain't got no hard feelings, but you didn't know
how that mantel had ought to be, so he done it
righd the other way, but he hadn't no righd to
talk to you like he done, nohow, and you was all
righd to send him away, but you might a shaked
hands, and none of the boys never said nothing
nor none of them never come to see him, 'cept
Carl Olsen, and that make him feel awful bad,
too! And when he feels so bad he don't no more
want to live, so I make him promise if I git him
back he never try to kill himself again. Oh, Mr.
Lossing, please don't let my man die!"

Bewildered and more touched than he cared to
feel, himself, Lossing still made a feeble stand for
discipline. "I don't see how Lieders can expect
me to take him back again," he began.

"He aint expecting you, Mr. Lossing, it's
me!"

"But didn't Lieders tell you I told him I would never take him back?"

"No, sir, no, Mr. Lossing, it was not that, it was you said it would be a cold day that you would take him back; and it was git so cold yesterday, so I think, 'Now it would be a cold day to-morrow and Mr. Lossing he can take Kurt back.' And it *is* the most coldest day this year!"

Lossing burst into a laugh, perhaps he was glad to have the Western sense of humor come to the rescue of his compassion. "Well, it was a cold day for you to come all this way for nothing," said he. "You go home and tell Lieders to report to-morrow."

Kurt's manner of receiving the news was characteristic. He snorted in disgust: "Well, I did think he had more sand than to give in to a woman!" But after he heard the whole story he chuckled: "Yes, it was that way he said, and he must do like he said; but that was a funny way you done, Thekla. Say, mamma, yesterday, was you look out for the cat or to find how cold it been?"

"Never you mind, papa," said Thekla, " you remember what you promised if I git you back?"

Lieders's eyes grew dull; he flung his arms out, with a long sigh. "No, I don't forget, I will keep my promise, but—it is like the handcuffs, Thekla, it is like the handcuffs!" In a second, however, he added, in a changed tone, "But thou art a kind jailer, mamma, more like a comrade. And no, it was not fair to thee—I know that now, Thekla."

THE FACE OF FAILURE

AFTER the week's shower the low Iowa hills looked vividly green. At the base of the first range of hills the Blackhawk road winds from the city to the prairie. From its starting-point, just outside the city limits, the wayfarer may catch bird's-eye glimpses of the city, the vast river that the Iowans love, and the three bridges tying three towns to the island arsenal. But at one's elbow spreads Cavendish's melon farm. Cavendish's melon farm it still is, in current phrase, although Cavendish, whose memory is honored by lovers of the cantaloupe melon, long ago departed to raise melons for larger markets; and still a weather-beaten sign creaks from a post announcing to the world that "the celebrated Cavendish Melons are for Sale here!" To-day the melon-vines were softly shaded by rain-drops. A pleasant sight they made, spreading for acres in front of the green-houses where mushrooms and early vegetables strove to outwit the seasons, and before the brown cottage in which Cavendish had begun a successful career. The black roof-tree of the cottage sagged in the middle, and the weather-boarding was dingy with the streaky dinginess of old paint that has never had enough oil. The fences, too, were unpainted and rudely patched. Nevertheless a second glance told one that there were no gaps in them, that the farm machines kept their bright colors well under cover, and that the garden rows were beautifully straight and clean. An old white horse switched its sleek sides with its long tail and drooped its untrammelled neck in front of the gate. The wagon to which it was harnessed was new and had just been washed. Near the gate stood a girl and boy who seemed to be mutually studying each other's person. Decidedly the girl's slim, light figure in its dainty frock repaid one's eyes for their trouble; and her face, with its brilliant violet eyes, its full, soft chin, its curling auburn hair and delicate tints, was charming; but her brother's look was anything but approving. His lip curled and his small gray eyes grew smaller under his scowling brows.

"Is *that* your best suit?" said the girl.

"Yes, it is; and it's *going* to be for one while," said the boy.

" Is that your best suit ? "

It was a suit of the cotton mixture that looks like wool when it is new, and cuts a figure on the counters of every dealer in cheap ready-made clothing. It had been Tim Powell's best attire for a year; perhaps he had not been careful enough of it, and that was why it no longer cared even to imitate wool; it was faded to the hue of a clay bank, it was threadbare, the trousers bagged at the knees, the jacket bagged at the elbows, the pockets bulged flabbily from sheer force of habit, although there was nothing in them.

"I thought you were to have a new suit," said the girl. "Uncle told me himself he was going to buy you one yesterday when you went to town."

"I wouldn't have asked him to buy me anything yesterday for more'n a suit of clothes."

"Why?" The girl opened her eyes. "Didn't he do anything with the lawyer? Is that why you are both so glum this morning?"

"No, he didn't. The lawyer says the woman that owns the mortgage has got to have the money. And it's due next week."

The girl grew pale all over her pretty rosy cheeks; her eyes filled with tears as she gasped, "Oh, how hateful of her, when she promised——"

"She never promised nothing, Eve; it ain't

been hers for more than three months. Sloan,
that used to have it, died, and left his property to
be divided up between his nieces; and the mortgage is her share. See?"

"I don't care, it's just as mean. Mr. Sloan
promised."

"No, he didn't; he jest said if Uncle was behind he wouldn't press him; and he did let Uncle
get behind with the interest two times and never
kicked. But he died; and now the woman, she
wants her money!"

"I think it is mean and cruel of her to turn us
out! Uncle says mortgages are wicked anyhow,
and I believe him!"

"I guess he couldn't have bought this place if
he didn't give a mortgage on it. And he'd have
had enough to pay cash, too, if Richards hadn't
begged him so to lend it to him."

"When is Richards going to pay him?"

"It come due three months ago; Richards
ain't never paid up the interest even, and now
he says he's got to have the mortgage extended
for three years; anyhow for two."

"But don't he *know* we've got to pay our own
mortgage? How can we help *him*? I wish
Uncle would sell him out!"

The boy gave her the superior smile of the masculine creature. " I suppose," he remarked with elaborate irony, " that he's like Uncle and you ; he thinks mortgages are wicked."

"And just as like as not Uncle won't want to go to the carnival," Eve went on, her eyes filling again.

Tim gazed at her, scowling and sneering ; but she was absorbed in dreams and hopes with which as yet his boyish mind had no point of contact.

" All the girls in the A class were going to go to see the fireworks together, and George Dean and some of the boys were going to take us, and we were going to have tea at May Arlington's house, and I was to stay all night ;"—this came in a half sob. " I think it is just too mean ! I never have any good times!"

" Oh, yes, you do, sis, lots ! Uncle always gits you everything you want. And he feels terrible bad when I—when he knows he can't afford to git something you want——"

" I know well enough who tells him we can't afford things ! "

" Well, do you want us to git things we can't afford? I ain't never advised him except the best I knew how. I told him Richards

4

was a blow-hard, and I told him those Alliance
grocery folks he bought such a lot of truck of
would skin him, and they did; those canned
things they sold him was all musty, and they
said there wasn't any freight on 'em, and he
had to pay freight and a fancy price besides;
and I don't believe they had any more to do
with the Alliance than our cow!"

"Uncle always believes everything. He
always is so sure things are going to turn out
just splendid; and they don't—only just mid-
dling; and then he loses a lot of money."

"But he is an awful good man," said the boy,
musingly.

"I don't believe in being so good you can't
make money. I don't want always to be poor
and despised, and have the other girls have
prettier clothes than me!"

"I guess you can be pretty good and yet
make money, if you are sharp enough. Of
course you got to be sharper to be good and
make money than you got to be, to be mean
and make money."

"Well, I know one thing, that Uncle ain't
ever going to make money. He——" The
last word shrivelled on her lips, which puckered

into a confused smile at the warning frown of
her brother. The man that they were discussing had come round to them past the hen-
house. How much had he overheard?

He didn't seem angry, anyhow. He called:
" Well, Evy, ready ? " and Eve was glad to run
into the house for her hat without looking at
him. It was a relief that she must sit on the
back seat where she need not face Uncle Nelson.
Tim sat in front ; but Tim was so stupid he
wouldn't mind.

Nor did he ; it was Nelson Forrest that stole
furtive glances at the lad's profile, the knitted
brows, the freckled cheeks, the undecided nose,
and firm mouth.

The boyish shoulders slouched forward at the
same angle as that of the fifty-year-old shoulders
beside him. Nelson, through long following of
the plough, had lost the erect carriage painfully
acquired in the army. He was a handsome man,
whose fresh-colored skin gave him a perpetual
appearance of having just washed his face. The
features were long and delicate. The brown eyes
had a liquid softness like the eyes of a woman.
In general the countenance was alertly intelli-
gent ; he looked younger than his years ; but this

afternoon the lines about his mouth and in his
brows warranted every gray hair of his pointed
short beard. There was a reason. Nelson was
having one of those searing flashes of insight that
do come occasionally to the most blindly hopeful
souls. Nelson had hoped all his life. He hoped
for himself, he hoped for the whole human race.
He served the abstraction that he called "*Progress*" with unflinching and unquestioning loy-
alty. Every new scheme of increasing happiness
by force found a helper, a fighter, and a giver in
him; by turns he had been an Abolitionist, a
Fourierist, a Socialist, a Greenbacker, a Farmers'
Alliance man. Disappointment always was followed hard on its heels by a brand-new confidence. Progress ruled his farm as well as his
politics; he bought the newest implements and
subscribed trustfully to four agricultural papers;
but being a born lover of the ground, a vein of
saving doubt did assert itself sometimes in his
work; and, on the whole, as a farmer he was
successful. But his success never ventured outside his farm gates. At buying or selling, at a
bargain in any form, the fourteen-year-old Tim
was better than Nelson with his fifty years' experience of a wicked and bargaining world.

Was that any part of the reason, he wondered to-day, why at the end of thirty years of unflinching toil and honesty, he found himself with a vast budget of experience in the ruinous loaning of money, with a mortgage on the farm of a friend, and a mortgage on his own farm likely to be foreclosed? Perhaps it might have been better to stay in Henry County. He had paid for his farm at last. He had known a good moment, too, that day he drove away from the lawyer's with the cancelled mortgage in his pocket and Tim hopping up and down on the seat for joy. But the next day Richards—just to give him the chance of a good thing—had brought out that Maine man who wanted to buy him out. He was anxious to put the money down for the new farm, to have no whip-lash of debt forever whistling about his ears as he ploughed, ready to sting did he stumble in the furrows; and Tim was more anxious than he; but—there was Richards! Richards was a neighbor who thought as he did about Henry George and Spiritualism, and belonged to the Farmers' Alliance, and had lent Nelson all the works of Henry George that he (Richards) could borrow. Richards was in deep trouble. He had lost his wife; he might lose his farm.

He appealed to Nelson, for the sake of old friend-
ship, to save him.   And Nelson could not resist ;
so, two thousand of the thirty-four hundred dollars that the Maine man paid went to Richards,
the latter swearing by all that is holy, to pay his
friend off in full at the end of the year.   There
was money coming to him from his dead wife's
estate, but it was tied up in the courts.   Nelson
would not listen to Tim's prophecies of evil.   But
he was a little dashed when Richards paid neither
interest nor principal at the year's end, although
he gave reasons of weight ; and he experienced
veritable consternation when the renewed mortgage ran its course and still Richards could not
pay.   The money from his wife's estate had been
used to improve his farm (Nelson knew how run-
down everything was), his new wife was sickly
and "didn't seem to take hold," there had been
a disastrous hail-storm—but why rehearse the
calamities ? they focussed on one sentence: it
was impossible to pay.

Then Nelson, who had been restfully count-
ing on the money from Richards for his own
debt, bestirred himself, only to find his patient
creditor gone and a woman in his stead who
must have her money.   He wrote again—

sorely against his will—begging Richards to raise
the money somehow. Richards's answer was
in his pocket, for he wore the best black broadcloth in which he had done honor to the lawyer, yesterday. Richards plainly was wounded;
but he explained in detail to Nelson how he
(Nelson) could borrow money of the banks on
his farm and pay Miss Brown. There was no
bank where Richards could borrow money;
and he begged Nelson not to drive his wife
and little children from their cherished home.
Nelson choked over the pathos when he read
the letter to Tim; but Tim only grunted a
wish that *he* had the handling of that feller.
And the lawyer was as little moved as Tim.
Miss Brown needed the money, he said. The
banks were not disposed to lend just at present; money, it appeared, was "tight;" so, in
the end, Nelson drove home with the face
of Failure staring at him between his horses'
ears.

There was only one way. Should he make
Richards suffer or suffer himself? Did a man
have to grind other people or be ground himself? Meanwhile they had reached the town.
The stir of a festival was in the air. On every

Money, it appeared, was "tight"

side bunting streamed in the breeze or was
draped across brick or wood. Arches spanned
some of the streets, with inscriptions of welcome
on them, and swarms of colored lanterns glittered against the sunlight almost as gayly as
they would show when they should be lighted
at night. Little children ran about waving
flags. Grocery wagons and butchers' wagons
trotted by with a flash of flags dangling from
the horses' harness. The streets were filled
with people in their holiday clothes. Everybody smiled. The shopkeepers answered questions and went out on the sidewalks to direct
strangers. From one window hung a banner
inviting visitors to enter and get a list of
hotels and boarding-houses. The crowd was
entirely good-humored and waited outside restaurants, bandying jokes with true Western
philosophy. At times the wagons made a
temporary blockade in the street, but no one
grumbled. Bands of music paraded past them,
the escort for visitors of especial consideration.
In a window belonging, the sign above de-
clared, to the Business Men's Association,
stood a huge doll clad in blue satin, on which
was painted a device of Neptune sailing down

the Mississippi amid a storm of fireworks. The doll stood in a boat arched about with lantern-decked hoops, and while Nelson halted, unable to proceed, he could hear the voluble explanation of the proud citizen who was interpreting to strangers.

This, Nelson thought, was success. Here were the successful men. The man who had failed looked at them. Eve roused him by a shrill cry, "There they are. There's May and the girls. Let me out quick, Uncle!"

He stopped the horse and jumped out himself to help her. It was the first time since she came under his roof that she had been away from it all night. He cleared his throat for some advice on behavior. "Mind and be respectful to Mrs. Arlington. Say yes, ma'am, and no, ma'am——" He got no further, for Eve gave him a hasty kiss and the crowd brushed her away.

"All she thinks of is wearing fine clothes and going with the fellers!" said her brother, disdainfully. "If I had to be born a girl, I wouldn't be born at all!"

"Maybe if you despise girls so, you'll be born a girl the next time," said Nelson. "Some folks thinks that's how it happens with us."

"Do *you*, Uncle?" asked Tim, running his mind forebodingly over the possible business results of such a belief. "S'posing he shouldn't be willing to sell the pigs to be killed, 'cause they might be some friends of his!" he reflected, with a rising tide of consternation.

Nelson smiled rather sadly. He said, in another tone: "Tim, I've thought so many things, that now I've about given up thinking. All I can do is to live along the best way I know how and help the world move the best I'm able."

"You bet *I* ain't going to help the world move," said the boy; "I'm going to look out for myself!"

"Then my training of you has turned out pretty badly, if that's the way you feel."

A little shiver passed over the lad's sullen face; he flushed until he lost his freckles in the red veil, and burst out passionately: "Well, I got eyes, ain't I? I ain't going to be bad, or drink, or steal, or do things to git put in the penitentiary; but I ain't going to let folks walk all over me like you do; no, sir!"

Nelson did not answer; in his heart he thought that he had failed with the children, too; and he

relapsed into that dismal study of the face of
Failure.

He had come to the city to show Tim the
sights, and, therefore, though like a man in a
dream, he drove conscientiously about the gay
streets, pointing out whatever he thought might
interest the boy, and generally discovering that
Tim had the new information by heart already.
All the while a question pounded itself, like the
beat of the heart of an engine, through the noise
and the talk: " Shall I give up Richards or be
turned out myself?"

When the afternoon sunlight waned he put up
the horse at a modest little stable where farmers
were allowed to bring their own provender. The
charges were of the smallest and the place neat
and weather-tight, but it had been a long time
before Nelson could be induced to use it, because
there was a higher-priced stable kept by an ex-
farmer and member of the Farmers' Alliance.
Only the fact that the keeper of the low-priced
stable was a poor orphan girl, struggling to earn
an honest livelihood, had moved him.

They had supper at a restaurant of Tim's dis-
covery, small, specklessly tidy, and as unexacting
of the pocket as the stable. It was an excellent

supper. But Nelson had no appetite ; in spite of
an almost childish capacity for being diverted, he
could attend to nothing but the question always
in his ears : " Richards or me—which ? "

Until it should be time for the spectacle they
walked down the hill, and watched the crowds
gradually blacken every inch of the river-banks.
Already the swarms of lanterns were beginning
to bloom out in the dusk. Strains of music
throbbed through the air, adding a poignant
touch to the excitement vibrating in all the faces
and voices about them. Even the stolid Tim felt
the contagion. He walked with a jaunty step
and assaulted a tune himself. " I tell you,
Uncle," says Tim, " it's nice of these folks to be
getting up all this show, and giving it for nothing ! "

" Do you think so ? " says Nelson. " You don't
love your book as I wish you did ; but I guess
you remember about the ancient Romans, and
how the great, rich Romans used to spend enormous sums in games and shows that they let the
people in free to—well, what for ? Was it to
learn them anything or to make them happy ?
Oh, no, it was to keep down the spirit of liberty,
Son, it was to make them content to be slaves !

Nelson had no appetite

And so it is here. These merchants and capital-
ists are only looking out for themselves, trying
to keep labor down and not let it know how
oppressed it is, trying to get people here from
everywhere to show what a fine city they have
and get their money."

" Well, *'tis* a fine town," Tim burst in, " a boss
town ! And they ain't gouging folks a little bit.
None of the hotels or the restaurants have put
up their prices one cent. Look what a dandy
supper we got for twenty-five cents ! And ain't
the boy at Lumley's grocery given me two tickets
to set on the steamboat ? There's nothing mean
about this town ! "

Nelson made no remark ; but he thought, for
the fiftieth time, that his farm was too near the
city. Tim was picking up all the city boys' false
pride as well as their slang. Unconscious Tim
resumed his tune. He knew that it was " Annie
Rooney " if no one else did, and he mangled the
notes with appropriate exhilaration.

Now, the river was as busy as the land, lights
swimming hither and thither ; steamboats with
ropes of tiny stars bespangling their dark bulk
and a white electric glare in the bow, low boats
with lights that sent wavering spear-heads into

the shadow beneath. The bridge was a blazing
barbed fence of fire, and beyond the bridge, at
the point of the island, lay a glittering multitude
of lights, a fairy fleet with miniature sails outlined in flame as if by jewels.

Nelson followed Tim. The crowds, the cease-
less clatter of tongues and jar of wheels, depressed
the man, who hardly knew which way to dodge
the multitudinous perils of the thoroughfare ; but
Tim used his elbows to such good purpose that
they were out of the levee, on the steamboat, and
settling themselves in two comfortable chairs in
a coign of vantage on deck, that commanded
the best obtainable view of the pageant, before
Nelson had gathered his wits together enough to
plan a path out of the crush.

"I sized up this place from the shore," Tim
sighed complacently, drawing a long breath of
relief ; "only jest two chairs, so we won't be
crowded."

Obediently, Nelson took his chair. His head
sank on his thin chest. Richards or himself,
which should he sacrifice? So the weary old
question droned through his brain. He felt a
tap on his shoulder. The man who roused him
was an acquaintance, and he stood smiling in the

5

attitude of a man about to ask a favor, while the
expectant half-smile of the lady on his arm
hinted at the nature of the favor. Would Mr.
Forrest be so kind?—there seemed to be no more
seats.   Before Mr. Forrest could be kind Tim
had yielded his own chair and was off, wriggling
among the crowd in search of another place.

"Smart boy, that youngster of yours," said the
man; "he'll make his way in the world, he can
push.   Well, Miss Alma, let me make you acquainted with Mr. Forrest. I know you will be
well entertained by him.   So, if you'll excuse
me, I'll get back and help my wife wrestle with
the kids.   They have been trying to see which
will fall overboard first ever since we came on
deck!"

Under the leeway of this pleasantry he bowed
and retired.   Nelson turned with determined
politeness to the lady.   He was sorry that she
had come, she looking to him a very fine lady
indeed, with her black silk gown, her shining
black ornaments, and her bright black eyes.   She
was not young, but handsome in Nelson's judgment, although of a haughty bearing.   "Maybe
she is the principal of the High School," thought
he.   "Martin has her for a boarder, and he said

she was very particular about her melons being
cold!"

But however formidable a personage, the lady
must be entertained.

"I expect you are a resident of the city,
ma'am?" said Nelson.

"Yes, I was born here." She smiled, a smile
that revealed a little break in the curve of her
cheek, not exactly a dimple, but like one.

"I don't know when I have seen such a fine
appearing lady," thought Nelson. He responded: "Well, I wasn't born here; but I come when
I was a little shaver of ten and stayed till I was
eighteen, when I went to Kansas to help fight
the border ruffians. I went to school here in the
Warren Street school-house."

"So did I, as long as I went anywhere to
school. I had to go to work when I was
twelve."

Nelson's amazement took shape before his
courtesy had a chance to control it. "I didn't
suppose you ever did any work in your life!"
cried he.

"I guess I haven't done much else. Father
died when I was twelve and the oldest of five,
the next only eight—Polly, that came between

Eb and me, died—naturally I had to work. I
was a nurse-girl by the day, first; and I never
shall forget how kind the woman was to me.
She gave me so much dinner I never needed to
eat any breakfast, which was a help."

"You poor little thing! I'm afraid you went
hungry sometimes." Immediately he marvelled
at his familiar speech, but she did not seem
to resent it.

"No, not so often," she said, musingly; "but I
used often and often to wish I could carry some
of the nice things home to mother and the babies.
After a while she would give me a cookey or a
piece of bread and butter for lunch; that I could
take home. I don't suppose I'll often have more
pleasure than I used to have then, seeing little Eb
waiting for sister; and the baby and mother——"
She stopped abruptly, to continue, in an instant,
with a kind of laugh; "I am never likely to feel
so important again as I did then, either. It was
great to have mother consulting me, as if I had
been grown up. I felt like I had the weight of
the nation on my shoulders, I assure you."

"And have you always worked since? You
are not working out now?" with a glance at her
shining gown.

"Oh, no, not for a long time. I learned to be a cook. I was a good cook, too, if I say it myself. I worked for the Lossings for four years. I am not a bit ashamed of being a hired girl, for I was as good a one as I knew how. It was Mrs. Lossing that first lent me books; and Harry Lossing, who is head of the firm now, got Ebenezer into the works. Ebenezer is shipping-clerk with a good salary and stock in the concern; and Ralph is there, learning the trade. I went to the business-college and learned book-keeping, and afterward I learned typewriting and shorthand. I have been working for the firm for fourteen years. We have educated the girls. Milly is married, and Kitty goes to the boarding-school, here."

"Then you haven't been married yourself?"

"What time did I have to think of being married? I had the family on my mind, and looking after them."

"That was more fortunate for your family than it was for my sex," said Nelson, gallantly. He accompanied the compliment by a glance of admiration, extinguished in an eye-flash, for the white radiance that had bathed the deck suddenly vanished.

"Now you will see a lovely sight," said the

woman, deigning no reply to his tribute; "listen! That is the signal."

The air was shaken with the boom of cannon. Once, twice, thrice. Directly the boat-whistles took up the roar, making a hideous din. The fleet had moved. Spouting rockets and Roman candles, which painted above it a kaleidoscopic archway of fire, welcomed by answering javelins of light and red and orange and blue and green flares from the shore; the fleet bombarded the bridge, escorted Neptune in his car, manœuvred and massed and charged on the blazing city with a many-hued shower of flame.

After the boats, silently, softly, floated the battalions of lanterns, so close to the water that they seemed flaming water-lilies, while the dusky mirror repeated and inverted their splendor.

"They're shingles, you know," explained Nelson's companion, "with lanterns on them; but aren't they pretty?"

"Yes, they are! I wish you had not told me. It is like a fairy story!"

"Ain't it? But we aren't through; there's more to come. Beautiful fireworks!"

The fireworks, however, were slow of coming. They could see the barge from which they were to be sent; they could watch the movements of the men in white oil-cloth who moved in a ghostly fashion about the barge; they could hear the tap of hammers; but nothing came of it all.

They sat in the darkness, waiting; and there came to Nelson a strange sensation of being alone and apart from all the breathing world with this woman. He did not perceive that Tim had quietly returned with a box which did very well for a seat, and was sitting with his knees against the chair-rungs. He seemed to be somehow outside of all the tumult and the spectacle. It was the vainglorying triumph of this world. He was the soul outside, the soul that had missed its triumph. In his perplexity and loneliness he felt an overwhelming longing for sympathy; neither did it strike Nelson, who believed in all sorts of occult influences, that his confidence in a stranger was unwarranted. He would have told you that his "psychic instincts" never played him false, although really they were traitors from their astral cradles to their astral graves.

He said in a hesitating way: "You must excuse me being kinder dull; I've got some serious business on my mind and I can't help thinking of it."

"Is that so? Well, I know how that is; I have often stayed awake nights worrying about things. Lest I shouldn't suit and all that—especially after mother took sick."

"I s'pose you had to give up and nurse her then?"

"That was what Ebenezer and Ralph were for having me do; but mother—my mother always had so much sense—mother says, 'No, Alma, you've got a good place and a chance in life, you sha'n't give it up. We'll hire a girl. I ain't never lonesome except evenings, and then you will be home. I should jest want to die,' she says, 'if I thought I kept you in a kind of prison like by my being sick—now, just when you are getting on so well.' There never *was* a woman like my mother!" Her voice shook a little, and Nelson asked gently:

"Ain't your mother living now?"

"No, she died last year." She added, after a little silence, "I somehow can't get used to being lonesome."

"It *is* hard," said Nelson. "I lost my wife three years ago."

"That's hard, too."

"My goodness! I guess it is. And it's hardest

when trouble comes on a man and he can't go
nowhere for advice."

"Yes, that's so, too. But -- have you any
children?"

"Yes, ma'am; that is, they ain't my own children. Lizzie and I never had any; but these
two we took and they are most like my own.
The girl is eighteen and the boy rising of fourteen."

"They must be a comfort to you; but they are
considerable of a responsibility, too."

"Yes, ma'am," he sighed softly to himself.
" Sometimes I feel I haven't done the right way
by them, though I've tried. Not that they ain't
good children, for they are—no better anywhere.
Tim, he will work from morning till night, and
never need to urge him; and he never gives me
a promise he don't keep it, no ma'am, never did
since he was a little mite of a lad. And he is a
kind boy, too, always good to the beasts; and
while he may speak up a little short to his sister,
he saves her many a step. He doesn't take to
his studies quite as I would like to have him, but
he has a wonderful head for business. There is
splendid stuff in Tim if it could only be worked
right."

While Nelson spoke, Tim was hunching his
shoulders forward in the darkness, listening with
the whole of two sharp ears. His face worked in
spite of him, and he gave an inarticulate snort.

"Well," the woman said, "I think that speaks
well for Tim. Why should you be worried about
him?"

"I am afraid he is getting to love money and
worldly success too well, and that is what I fear
for the girl, too. You see, she is so pretty, and
the idols of the tribe and the market, as Bacon
calls them, are strong with the young."

"Yes, that's so," the woman assented vaguely,
not at all sure what either Bacon or his idols
might be. "Are the children relations of
yours?"

"No, ma'am; it was like this: When I was up
in Henry County there came a photographic artist to the village near us, and pitched his tent
and took tintypes in his wagon. He had his
wife and his two children with him. The poor
woman fell ill and died; so we took the two
children. My wife was willing; she was a won-
derfully good woman, member of the Methodist
church till she died. I—I am not a church member myself, ma'am; I passed through that stage

... There came a photographic artist to the village.

of spiritual development a long while ago." He
gave a wistful glance at his companion's dimly
outlined profile. "But I never tried to disturb
her faith; it made *her* happy."

"Oh, I don't think it is any good fooling with
other people's religions," said the woman, easily.
"It is just like trying to talk folks out of drink-
ing; nobody knows what is right for anybody
else's soul any more than they do what is good
for anybody else's stomach!"

"Yes, ma'am. You put things very clearly."

"I guess it is because you understand so
quickly. But you were saying——"

"That's all the story. We took the children,
and their father was killed by the cars the next
year, poor man; and so we have done the best we
could ever since by them."

"I should say you had done very well by
them."

"No, ma'am; I haven't done very well somehow by anyone, myself included, though God
knows I've tried hard enough!"

Then followed the silence natural after such a
confession when the listener does not know the
speaker well enough to parry abasement by
denial.

"I am impressed," said Nelson, simply, "to talk with you frankly. It isn't polite to bother strangers with your troubles, but I am impressed that you won't mind."

"Oh, no, I won't mind."

It was not extravagant sympathy; but Nelson thought how kind her voice sounded, and what a musical voice it was. Most people would have called it rather sharp.

He told her—with surprisingly little egotism, as the keen listener noted—the story of his life; the struggle of his boyhood; his random self-education; his years in the army (he had criticised his superior officers, thereby losing the promotion that was coming for bravery in the field); his marriage (apparently he had married his wife because another man had jilted her); his wrestle with nature (whose pranks included a cyclone) on a frontier farm that he eventually lost, having put all his savings into a "Greenback" newspaper, and being thus swamped with debt; his final slow success in paying for his Iowa farm; and his purchase of the new farm, with its resulting disaster. "I've farmed in Kansas," he said, "in Nebraska, in Dakota, in Iowa. I was willing to go wherever the land promised. It always seemed like I was

going to succeed, but somehow I never did. The
world ain't fixed right for the workers, I take it.
A man who has spent thirty years in hard, honest
toil oughtn't to be staring ruin in the face like I
am to-day. They won't let it be so when we have
the single tax and when we farmers send our own
men instead of city lawyers, to the Legislature
and halls of Congress. Sometimes I think it's
the world that's wrong and sometimes I think it's
me!"

The reply came in crisp and assured accents,
which were the strongest contrast to Nelson's
soft, undecided pipe: "Seems to me in this last
case the one most to blame is neither you nor the
world at large, but this man Richards, who is asking *you* to pay for *his* farm. And I notice you
don't seem to consider your creditor in this business. How do you know she don't need the
money? Look at me, for instance; I'm in some
financial difficulty myself. I have a mortgage for
two thousand dollars, and that mortgage—for
which good value was given, mind you—falls due
this month. I want the money. I want it bad.
I have a chance to put my money into stock at
the factory. I know all about the investment;
I haven't worked there all these years and not

know how the business stands. It is a chance
to make a fortune. I ain't likely to ever have
another like it ; and it won't wait for me to make
up my mind forever, either. Isn't it hard on me,
too?"

"Lord knows it is, ma'am," said Nelson, de-
spondently ; "it is hard on us all! Sometimes I
don't see the end of it all. A vast social revolution——"

"Social fiddlesticks! I beg your pardon, Mr.
Forrest, but it puts me out of patience to have
people expecting to be allowed to make every
mortal kind of fools of themselves and then have
'a social revolution' jump in to slue off the con-
sequences. Let us understand each other. Who
do you suppose I am?"

"Miss—Miss Almer, ain't it?"

"It's Alma Brown, Mr. Forrest. I saw you
coming on the boat and I made Mr. Martin fetch
me over to you. I told him not to say my name,
because I wanted a good plain talk with you.
Well, I've had it. Things are just about where
I thought they were, and I told Mr. Lossing so.
But I couldn't be sure. You must have thought
me a funny kind of woman to be telling you all
those things about myself."

Nelson, who had changed color half a dozen times in the darkness, sighed before he said: " No, ma'am; I only thought how good you were to tell me. I hoped maybe you were impressed to trust me as I was to trust you."

Being so dark Nelson could not see the queer expression on her face as she slowly shook her head. She was thinking: "If I ever saw a babe in arms trying to do business! How did *he* ever pay for a farm?" She said: " Well, I did it on purpose; I wanted you to know I wasn't a cruel aristocrat, but a woman that had worked as hard as yourself. Now, why shouldn't you help me and yourself instead of helping Richards? You have confidence in me, you say. Well, show it. I'll give you your mortgage for your mortgage on Richards's farm. Come, can't you trust Richards to me? You think it over."

The hiss of a rocket hurled her words into space. The fireworks had begun. Miss Brown looked at them and watched Nelson at the same time. As a good business woman who was also a good citizen, having subscribed five dollars to the carnival, she did not propose to lose the worth of her money; neither did she intend to lose a chance to do business. Perhaps there was an obscurer and more complex motive lurking in some stray corner of that queer garret, a woman's mind. Such motives—aimless softenings of the heart, unprofitable diversions of the fancy—will seep unconsciously through the toughest business principles of woman.

She was puzzled by the look of exaltation on Nelson's features, illumined as they were by the uncanny light. If the fool man had not forgotten all his troubles just to see a few fireworks! No, he was not that kind of a fool; maybe—and she almost laughed aloud in her pleasure over her own insight — maybe it all made him think of the war, where he had been so brave. "He was a regular hero in the war," Miss Brown concluded, "and he certainly is a perfect gentleman; what a pity he hasn't got any sense!"

She had guessed aright, although she had not guessed deep enough in regard to Nelson. He watched the great wheels of light, he watched the river aflame with Greek fire, then, with a shiver, he watched the bombs bursting into myriads of flowers, into fizzing snakes, into fields of burning gold, into showers of jewels that made the night splendid for a second and faded. They

6

were not fireworks to him ; they were a magi-
cal phantasmagoria that renewed the incoherent
and violent emotions of his youth ; again he was
in the chaos of the battle, or he was dreaming by
his camp-fire, or he was pacing his lonely round
on guard. His heart leaped again with the old
glow, the wonderful, beautiful worship of Liberty
that can do no wrong. He seemed to hear a
thousand voices chanting :

" In the beauty of the lilies Christ was born across the sea,
    As He died to make men holy, let us die to make men free !"

His turbid musings cleared—or they seemed
to him to clear—under the strong reaction of
his imagination and his memories. It was all
over, the dream and the glory thereof. The
splendid young soldier was an elderly, ruined
man. But one thing was left : he could be true
to his flag.

" A poor soldier, but enlisted for the war," says
Nelson, squaring his shoulders, with a lump in his
throat and his eyes brimming. " I know by the
way it hurts me to think of refusing her that it's
a temptation to wrong-doing. No, I can't save
myself by sacrificing a brother soldier for hu-
manity. She is just as kind as she can be, but

women don't understand business; she wouldn't make allowance for Richards."

He felt a hand on his shoulder; it was Martin apologizing for hurrying Miss Brown; but the baby was fretting and——

"I'm sorry—yes—well, I wish you didn't have to go!" Nelson began; but a hoarse treble rose from under his elbows: "Say, Mr. Martin, Uncle and me can take Miss Brown home."

"If you will allow me the pleasure," said Nelson, with the touch of courtliness that showed through his homespun ways.

"Well, I *would* like to see the hundred bombs bursting at once and Vulcan at his forge!" said Miss Brown.

Thus the matter arranged itself. Tim waited with the lady while Nelson went for the horse, nor was it until afterward that Miss Brown wondered why the lad did not go instead of the man. But Tim had his own reasons. No sooner was Nelson out of earshot than he began: "Say, Miss Brown, I can tell you something."

"Yes?"

"That Richards is no good; but you can't get Uncle to see it. At least it will take time. If you'll help me we can get him round in time.

Won't you please not sell us out for six months
and give me a show? I'll see you get your interest and your money, too."

"You?" Miss Brown involuntarily took a
business attitude, with her arms akimbo, and
eyed the boy.

"Yes, ma'am, me. I ain't so very old, but I
know all about the business. I got all the figures
down—how much we raise and what we got last
year. I can fetch them to you so you can see.
He is a good farmer, and he will catch on to the
melons pretty quick. We'll do better next year,
and I'll try to keep him from belonging to things
and spending money; and if he won't lend to
anybody or start in raising a new kind of crop
just when we get the melons going, he will make
money sure. He is awful good and honest. All
the trouble with him is he needs somebody to
take care of him. If Aunt Lizzie had been alive
he never would have lent that dead-beat Richards
that money. He ought to get married."

Miss Brown did not feel called on to say anything. Tim continued in a judicial way: "He is
awful good and kind, always gets up in the morning to make the fire if I have got something else
to do; and he'd think everything his wife did was

the best in the world; and if he had somebody
to take care of him he'd make money. I don't
suppose *you*
would think
of it?" This
last in an
insinuating
tone, with
evident anx-
iety.

"Well, I
never!" said
Miss Brown.

Whether
she was more
offended or
amused she
couldn't
tell; and she
stood star-
ing at him
by the elec-
tric light.

"Well, I never!" said Miss Brown.

To her amazement the hard little face began to
twitch. "I didn't mean to mad you," Tim
grunted, with a quiver in his rough voice. "I've

been listening to every word you said, and I
thought you were so sensible you'd talk over
things without nonsense. Of course I knew he'd
have to come and see you Saturday nights, and
take you buggy riding, and take you to the thea-
tre, and all such things—first. But I thought we
could sorter fix it up between ourselves. I've
taken care of him ever since Aunt Lizzie died,
and I did my best he shouldn't lend that money,
but I couldn't help it ; and I did keep him from
marrying a widow woman with eight children,
who kept telling him how much her poor
fatherless children needed a man ; and I never
did see anybody I was willing—before—and
it's—it's so lonesome without Aunt Lizzie!"
He choked and frowned. Poor Tim, who had
sold so many melons to women and seen so
much of back doors and kitchen humors that
he held the sex very cheap, he did not realize
how hard he would find it to talk of the one
woman who had been kind to him! He
turned red with shame over his own weakness.

"You poor little chap!" cried Miss Brown ;
"you poor little sharp, innocent chap!" The
hand she laid on his shoulder patted it as she
went on : "Never mind, if I can't marry your

uncle, I can help you take care of him. You're a real nice boy, and I'm not mad; don't you think it. There's your uncle now."

Nelson found her so gentle that he began to have qualms lest his carefully prepared speech should hurt her feelings. But there was no help for it now. " I have thought over your kind offer to me, ma'am," said he, humbly, " and I got a proposition to make to you. It is your honest due to have your farm, yes, ma'am. Well, I know a man would like to buy it; I'll sell it to him, and pay you your money."

" But that wasn't my proposal."

" I know it, ma'am. I honor you for your kindness; but I can't risk what—what might be another person's idea of duty about Richards. Our consciences ain't all equally enlightened, you know."

Miss Brown did not answer a word.

They drove along the streets where the lanterns were fading. Tim grew uneasy, she was silent so long. On the brow of the hill she indicated a side street and told them to stop the horse before a little brown house. One of the windows was a dim square of red.

" It isn't quite so lonesome coming home to a light," said Miss Brown.

As Nelson cramped the wheel to jump out to help her from the vehicle, the light from the electric arc fell full on his handsome face and showed her the look of compassion and admiration, there.

" Wait one moment," she said, detaining him with one firm hand. " I've got something to say to you. Let Richards go for the present; all I ask of you about him is that you will do nothing until we can find out if he is so bad off. But, Mr. Forrest. I can do better for you about that mortgage. Mr. Lossing will take it for three years for a relative of his and pay me the money. I told him the story."

" And *you* will get the money all right?"

" Just the same. I was only trying to help you a little by the other way, and I failed. Never mind."

" I can't tell you how you make me feel," said Nelson.

" Please let him bring you some melons to-morrow and make a stagger at it, though," said Tim.

" Can I ? " Nelson's eyes shone.

"If you want to," said Miss Brown. She laughed; but in a moment she smiled.

All the way home Nelson saw the same face of Failure between the old mare's white ears; but its grim lineaments were softened by a smile, a smile like Miss Brown's.

TOMMY AND THOMAS

IT was while Harry Lossing was at the High School that Mrs. Carriswood first saw Tommy Fitzmaurice. He was not much to see, a long lad of sixteen who had outgrown his jackets and was not yet grown to his ears.

At this period Mrs. Fitzmaurice was his barber, and she, having been too rash with the shears in one place, had snipped off the rest of his curly black locks "to match;" until he showed a perfect convict's poll, giving his ears all the better chance, and bringing out the rather square contour of his jaws to advantage. He had the true Irish-Norman face; a skin of fine texture, fair and freckled, high cheekbones, straight nose, and wide blue eyes that looked to be drawn with ink, because of their sharply pencilled brows and long, thick, black lashes. But the feature that Mrs. Carriswood noticed was Tommy's mouth, a flexible and

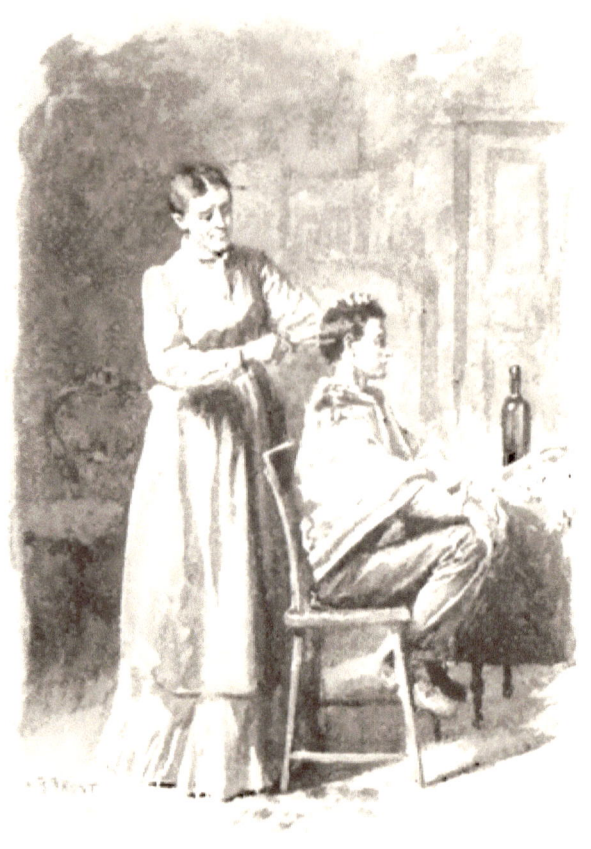

At this period Mrs. Fitzmaurice was his barber.

delicately cut mouth, of which the lips moved lightly in speaking and seldom were quite in repose.

" The genuine Irish orator's mouth," thought Mrs. Carriswood.

Tommy, however, was not a finished orator, and Mrs. Carriswood herself deigned to help him with his graduating oration; Tommy delivering the aforesaid oration from memory, on the stage of the Grand Opera House, to a warm-hearted and perspiring audience of his towns-people, amid tremendous applause and not the slightest proddings of conscience.

Really the speech deserved the applause ; Mrs. Carriswood, who had heard half the eloquence of the world, spent three evenings on it ; and she has a good memory.

Her part in the affair always amused her ; though, in fact, it came to pass easily. She had the great fortune of the family. Being a widow with no children, and the time not being come when philanthropy beckons on the right hand and on the left to free-handed women, Mrs. Carriswood travelled. As she expressed it, she was searching the globe for a perfect climate. " Not that I in the least expect to find it," said she, cheerfully, " but I like to vary my disappointments ; when I get worn out being frozen, winters, I go somewhere to be soaked." She was on

her way to California this time, with her English
maid, who gave the Lossing domestics many a
jolly moment by her inextinguishable panic about
red Indians. Mrs. Derry supposed these savages
to be lurking on the prairie outside every Western town; and almost fainted when she did

Three Kickapoo Indians, splendid in paint and feathers, peacefully
vending the "Famous Kickapoo Sagwa."

chance to turn the corner upon three Kickapoo
Indians, splendid in paint and feathers, and
peacefully vending the "Famous Kickapoo Sagwa." She had others of the artless notions of
the travelling English, and I fear that they were
encouraged not only by the cook, the "second
girl," and the man-of-all-work, but by Harry and

his chum, Tommy ; I know she used to tell how
she saw tame buffalo "roosting" on the streets,
"w'ich they do look that like common cows a
body couldn't tell 'em hapart!"

She had a great opinion of Tommy, a mystery
to her mistress for a long time, until one day it
leaked out that Tommy "and Master Harry,
too," had told her that Tommy's great-grandfather was a lord in the old country.

"The family seem to have sunk in the world
since, Derry," was Mrs. Carriswood's single remark, as she smiled to herself. After Derry was
dismissed she picked up a letter, written that day
to a friend of hers, and read some passages about
Harry and Tommy, smiling again.

"Harry"—one may look over her pretty
shoulder without impertinence, in a story—
"Harry," she wrote, "is a boy that I long to
steal. Just the kind of boy we have both
wanted, Sarah — frank, happy, affectionate. I
must tell you something about him. It came
out by accident. He has the Western business
instincts, and what do you suppose he did? He
actually started a wee shop of his own in the
corner of the yard (really it is a surprisingly
pretty place, and they are quite civilized in the

house, gas, hot water, steam heat, all most comfortable), and sold 'pop' and candy and cakes to the boys. He made so much money that he proposed a partnership to the cook and the setting up a little booth in the 'county fair,' which is like our rural cattle shows, you know. The cook (a superior person who borrows books from Mrs. Lossing, but seems very decent and respectful notwithstanding, and broils game to perfection. And *such* game as we have here, Sarah!) well, the cook made him cream-cakes, sandwiches, tarts, and candy, and Harry honorably bought all the provisions with his profits from the first venture. You will open your eyes at his father permitting such a thing, but Henry Lossing is a thorough Westerner in some ways, and he looks on it all as a joke. 'Might show the boy how to do business,' he says.

"Well, they had a ravishing display, so Alma, the cook, and William, the man, assured me—per Derry. All the sadder its fate; for alas! a gang of rowdy boys fell upon Harry, and while he was busy fighting half of them—he is as plucky as his uncle, the general—the other half looted the beautiful stock in trade! They would have despoiled our poor little merchant entirely but for

the opportune arrival of a schoolmate who is
mightily respected by the rowdies. He knocked
one of them down and shouted after the others
that he would give every one of them a good
thrashing if they did not bring the plunder back;
and as he is known to be a lad of his word for
good or evil, actually the scamps did return most
of the booty, which the two boys brushed off and
sold, as far as it went (!)   The consequence of the
fray has been that Harry is unboundedly grateful
to this Tommy Fitzmaurice, and is at present
coaching him on his graduating oration. Fitzmaurice has studied hard and won honors, and
wants to make a show with his oration, to please
his father. 'You see,' says Harry, 'Tommy's
father has saved money and is spending it all on
Tommy, so's he can be educated. He needs
Tommy in the business real bad, but he won't
let him come in; he keeps him at school, and he
thinks everything of his getting the valedictory,
and Tommy, he worked nights studying to get it.'
When I asked what was the father's business,
Harry grew a bit confused. 'Well, he kept a
saloon; but'—Harry hastened to explain—'it
was a very nice saloon, never any trouble with the
police there; why, Tommy knew every man on

the force. And they keep good liquors, too,' said Harry, earnestly; ' throw away all the beer left in the glasses.' ' What else would they do with it?' asked innocent I. ' Why, keep it in a bucket,' said Harry, solemnly, 'and then slip the glass under the counter and half fill out of the bucket, then hold it under the keg *low*, so's the foam will come; that's a trick of the trade, you know. Tommy says his father would *scorn* that!' There is a vista opened, isn't there? I was rather shocked at such associates for Harry, and told his mother. Did she think it a good idea to have such a boy coming to the house? a saloon-keeper's son? She did not laugh, as I half expected, but answered quite seriously that she had been looking up Tommy, that he was very much attached to Harry, and that she did not think he would teach him anything bad. He has, I find myself, notions of honor, though they are rather the code of the street. And he picks up things quickly. Once he came to tea. It was amusing to see how he glued his eyes on Harry and kept time with his motions. He used his fork quite properly, only as Harry is a left-handed little fellow, the right-handed Thomas had the more difficulty.

7

" He is taking such vast pains with his 'oration'
that I felt moved to help him. The subject is
'The Triumph of Democracy,' and Tommy civilly
explained that 'democracy' did not mean the
Democratic party, but 'just only a government
where all the poor folks can get their rights and
can vote.'

" The oration was the kind of spread-eagle
thing you might expect; I can see that Tommy
has formed himself on the orators of his father's
respectable saloon. What he said in comment
interested me more. 'Sure, I guess it is the best
government, ma'am, though, of course, I got to
make it out that way, anyhow. But we come
from Ireland, and there they got the other kind,
and me granny, she starved in the famine time,
she did that—with the fever. Me father walked
twenty mile to the Sackville's place, where they
gave him some meal, though he wasn't one of
their tenants; yes, and the lady told him how he
would be cooking it. I never will forget that
lady!'

" I saw a dramatic opportunity: would Tommy
be willing to tell that story in his speech? He
looked at me with an odd look—or so I imagined
it! 'Why not?' says he; 'I'd as soon as not tell

it to anyone of them, and why not to them all together?' Well, why not, when you come to think of it? So we have got it into the speech; and I, I myself, Sarah, am drilling young Demosthenes, and he is so apt a scholar that I find myself rather pleasantly employed." Having read her letter, Mrs. Carriswood hesitated a second and then added Derry's information at the bottom of the page. " I suppose the lordly ancestor was one of King James's creation—see Macaulay, somewhere in the second volume. I dare say there is a drop or two of good blood in the boy. He has the manners of a gentleman—but I don't know that I ever saw an Irishman, no matter how low in the social scale, who hadn't."

Thus it happened that Tommy's valedictory scored a success that is a tradition of the High School, and came to be printed in both the city papers; copies of which journals Tommy's mother has preserved sacredly to this day; and I have no doubt, could one find them, they would be found wrapped around a yellow photograph of the " A Class " of 1870: eight pretty girls in white, smiling among five solemn boys in black, and Tommy himself, as the valedictorian, occupying the centre of the picture in his new suit of broadcloth, with

a rose in his buttonhole and his hair cut by a professional barber for the occasion.

It was the story of the famine that really capt-

Tommy's valedictory.

ured the audience; and Tommy told it well,
with the true Irish fire, in a beautiful voice.

In the front seat of the parquette a little old
man in a wrinkled black broadcloth, with a bald

head and a fringe of whisker under his long chin, and a meek little woman, in a red Paisley shawl, wept and laughed by turns. They had taken the deepest interest in every essay and every speech. The old man clapped his large hands (which were encased in loose, black kid gloves) with unflagging vigor. He wore a pair of heavy boots, the soles of which made a noble thud on the floor.

"Ain't it wonderful the like of them young craters can talk like that!" he cried; "shure, Molly, that young lady who'd the essay—where is it?"—a huge black forefinger travelled down the page—"'*Music, The Turkish Patrol.*' No—though that's grand, that piece; I'll be spakin' wid Professor Von Keinmitz to bring it when we've the opening. Here 'tis, Molly: '*Tin, Essay. The Darkest Night Brings Out the Stars, Miss Mamie Odenheimer.*' Thrue for you, mavourneen! And the sintiments, wasn't they illigant? and the langwidge was as foine as Pat Ronan's speeches or Father—whist! will ye look at the flowers that shlip of a gyirl's gitting! Count 'em, will ye?"

"Fourteen bouquets and wan basket," says the little woman, "and Mamie Odenheimer, she got seventeen bouquets and two baskets and a sign.

Well," she looked anxious, but smiled, " I know of siven bouquets Tommy will git for sure. And that's not countin' what Harry Lossing will do for him. Hiven bless the good heart of him!"

" Well, I kin count four for him on wan seat," says the man, with a nod of his head toward the gay heap in the woman's lap, " barrin' I ain't onvaygled into flinging some of thim to the young ladies!"

Harry Lossing, in the seat behind with his mother and Mrs. Carriswood, giggled at this and whispered in the latter lady's ear, " That's Tommy's father and mother. My, aren't they excited, though! And Tommy's white's a sheet—for fear he'll disappoint them, you know. He has said his piece over twice to me, to-day, he's so scared lest he'll forget. I've got it in my pocket, and I'm going behind when it's his turn, to prompt him. Did you see me winking at him? it sort of cheers him up."

He was almost as keen over the floral procession as the Fitzmaurices themselves. The Lossing garden had been stripped to the last bud, and levies made on the asparagus-bed, into the bargain, and Mrs. Lossing and Alma and Mrs. Carriswood and Derry and Susy Lossing had made

bouquets and baskets and wreaths, and Harry
had distributed them among friends in different
parts of the house. I say Harry, but, complimented by Mrs. Carriswood, he admitted ingenu-
ously that it was Tommy's idea.

" Tommy thought they would make more show
that way," says Harry, " and they are all on the
middle aisle, so his father and mother can see
them ; Tim O'Halloran has got one for him, too,
and Mrs. Macillarney, and she's got some splendid pinies. Picked every last one. They'll make
a show!"

But Harry knew nothing of the most magnifi-
cent of his friend's trophies until it undulated
gloriously down the aisle, above the heads of
two men, white satin ribbons flying, tinfoil shining—an enormous horseshoe of roses and mig-
nonette !

The parents were both on their feet to crane
their necks after it, as it passed them amid the
plaudits.

" Oh, it was *you*, Cousin Margaret ; I know it
was you," cried Harry.

He took the ladies over to the Fitzmaurices
the minute that the diplomas were given ; and,
directly, Tommy joined them, attended by two

admiring followers laden with the trophies. Mrs.
O'Halloran and Mrs. Macillarney and divers of
the friends, both male and female, joined the
circle. Tommy held quite a little court. He
shook hands with all the ladies, beginning with
Mrs. Carriswood (who certainly never had found
herself before in such a company, jammed between Alderman McGinnis's resplendent new
tweeds and Mrs. Macillarney's calico); he affectionately embraced his mother, and he allowed
himself to be embraced by Mrs. Macillarney and
Mrs. O'Halloran, while Patrick Fitzmaurice shook
hands with the alderman.

" Here's the lady that helped me on me piece,
father ; she's the lady that sent me the horseshoe, mother. Like to make you acquainted with
me father and me mother. Mr. and Mrs. Fitzmaurice, Mrs. Carriswood."

In these words, Tommy, blushing and happy,
presented his happy parents.

" Sure, I'm proud to meet you, ma'am," said
Fitzmaurice, bowing, while his wife courtesied
and wiped her eyes.

They were very grateful, but they were more
grateful for the flowers than for the oratorical
drilling. No doubt they thought that their

Tommy could have done as well in any case; but the splendid horseshoe was another matter!

Ten years passed before Mrs. Carriswood saw her pupil again. During those years the town had increased and prospered; so had the Lossing Art Furniture Works. It was after Harry Lossing had disappointed his father. This is not saying that he had done anything out of the way; he had simply declined to be the fourth Harry Lossing on the rolls of Harvard College. Instead, he proposed to enter the business and to begin by learning his own trade. He was so industrious, he kept at it with such energy that his first convert was his father—no, I am wrong, Mrs. Carriswood was the first; Mrs. Lossing was not a convert, *she* had believed in Harry from the beginning. But all this was years before Mrs. Carriswood's visit.

Another of Master Harry's notions was his belief in the necessity of his " meddling "—so his father put it—in the affairs of the town, the state, and the nation, as well as those of the Lossing furniture company. But, though he was pleased to make rather cynical fun of his son's political enthusiasm, esteeming it in a sense a diverting and therefore reprehensible pursuit for a business

man, the elder Lossing had a sneaking pride in it,
all the same. He liked to bring out Harry's
political shrewdness.

"Fancy, Margaret," says he, "whom do you
think Harry has brought over to our side now?
The shrewdest ward politician in the town—why,
you saw him when he was a boy—Tommy Fitzmaurice."

Then Mrs. Carriswood remembered ; she asked,
amused, how was Tommy and where was he?

"Tommy? Oh, he went to the State university ; the old man was bound to send him, and he
was more dutiful than some sons. He was grad-
uated with honors, and came back to a large,
ready-made justice court's practice. Of course he
drifted into criminal practice ; but he has made a
fine income out of that, and is the shrewdest,
some folks say the least scrupulous, political
manager in the county. And so, Harry, you
have persuaded him to cast in his lot with the
party of principle, have you? and he is packing
the primaries?"

"I see nothing dishonest in our trying to
get our friends out to vote at the primaries,
sir."

"Of course not, but he may not stop there.

However, I want Bailey elected, and I am glad he will work for us; what's his price?"

Harry blushed a little. "I believe he would like to be city attorney, sir," said he; and Mr. Lossing laughed.

"Would he make a bad one?" asked Mrs. Carriswood.

"He would make the best kind of a one," replied Harry, with youthful fervor; "he's a ward politician and all that, I know; but he has it in him to be an uncommon deal more! And I say, sir, do you know that he and the old man will take twenty-five thousand of the stock at par if we turn ourselves into a corporation?"

"How about this new license measure? won't that bear a little bit hard on the old man?" This from Mr. Lossing, who was biting his cigar in deep thought.

"That will not prevent his doing his duty; why, the old man for very pride will be the first to obey the law. You'll *see!*"

Six months later they did see, since it was mostly due to Fitzmaurice's efforts that the reform candidate was elected; as a consequence, Tommy became prosecuting attorney; and, to the amazement of the critics, made the best prosecuting attorney that the city had ever known.

It was during the campaign that Mrs. Carriswood met him. Her goddaughter, daughter of the friend to whom years ago she described Tommy, was with her. This time Mrs. Carriswood had recently added Florida to her disappointments in climates, and was back, as she told Mrs. Lossing, " with a real sense of relief in a climate that was too bad to make any pretensions."

She had brought Miss Van Harlem to see the shops. It may be that she would not have been averse to Harry Lossing's growing interested in young Margaret. She had seen a great deal of Harry while he was East at school, and he remained her first favorite, while Margaret was as good as she was pretty, and had half a million of dollars in her own right. They had seen Harry, and he was showing them through the different buildings or " shops," when a man entered who greeted him cordially, and whom he presented to Mrs. Carriswood. It was Tommy Fitzmaurice, grown into a handsome young man. He brought his heels together and made the ladies a solemn bow. " Pleased to meet you, ladies; how do you like the West?" said Tommy.

His black locks curled about his ears, which seemed rather small now; he had a good nose and a mobile, clean-shaven face. His hands were very white and soft, and the rim of linen above them was dazzling. His black frock-coat was buttoned snugly about his slim waist. He brushed his face with a fine silk handkerchief, and thereby diffused the fragrance of the best imported cologne among the odors of wood and turpentine. A diamond pin sparkled from his neckscarf. The truth is, he knew that the visitors were coming and had made a state toilet. " He looks half like an actor and half like a clergyman, and he *is* all a politician," thought Mrs. Carriswood; " I don't think I shall like him any more." While she thought, she was inclining her slender neck toward him, and the gentlest interest and pleasure beamed out of her beautiful, dark eyes.

" We like the West, but *I* have liked it for ten years; this is not my first visit," said Mrs. Carriswood.

" I have reason to be glad for that, madam. I never made another speech so good."

He had remembered her; she laughed. "I had thought that you would forget."

"How could I, when you have not changed at all?"

"But you have," says Mrs. Carriswood, hardly knowing whether to show the young man his place or not.

"Yes, ma'am, naturally. But I have not learned how to make a speech yet."

"Ah, but you make very good ones, Harry tells me."

"Much obliged, Harry. No, ma'am, Harry is a nice boy; but he doesn't know. I know there is a lot to learn, and I guess a lot to unlearn; and I feel all outside; I don't even know how to get at it. I have wished a thousand times that I could talk with the lady who taught me to speak in the first place." He walked on by her side, talking eagerly. "You don't know how many times I have felt I would give most anything for the opportunity of just seeing you and talking with you; those things you said to me I always remembered." He had a hundred questions evidently stinging his tongue. And some of them seemed to Mrs. Carriswood very apposite.

"I'm on the outside of such a lot of things,"
says he. "When I first began to suspect that
I was on the outside was when I went to the
High School, and sometimes I was invited to
Harry's; that was my first acquaintance with
cultivated society. You can't learn manners
from books, ma'am. I learned them at Harry's.
That is,"—he colored and laughed,—"I learned
some. There's plenty left, I know. Then, I
went to the University. Some of the boys came
from homes like Harry's, and some of the professors there used to ask us to their houses; and
I saw engravings and oil paintings, and heard
the conversation of persons of culture. All this
only makes me know enough to *know* I am outside. I can see the same thing with the lawyers,
too. There is a set of them that are after
another kind of things; that think themselves
above me and my sort of fellows. You know all
the talk about this being a free and equal country. That's the tallest kind of humbug, madam!
It is that. There are sets, one above another,
everywhere; big bugs and little bugs, if you will
excuse the expression. And you can't influence
the big ones without knowing how they feel. A
fellow can't be poking in the dark in a speech or

anywhere else.   Now, these fellows here, they go
into politics, sometimes; and there, I tell you, we
come the nearest to a fair field and no favor!   It
is the best fellow gets the prize there—the sharp-
est-witted, the nerviest, and stanchest.   Oh, talk
of machine politics! all the soft chaps who ain't
willing to get up early in the morning, or to go
out in the wet, *they* howl about the primaries and
corruption; let them get up and clean the primaries instead of holding their noses!   Those
fellows, I'm not nice enough for them, but I can
beat them every time.   They make a monstrous
racket in the newspapers, but when election
comes on they can't touch side, edge, or bottom!"

Discoursing in this fashion, with digressions to
Harry in regard to the machines, the furniture,
and the sales, that showed Mrs. Carriswood that
he meant to keep an eye on his twenty odd
thousand dollars, he strolled at her side.   To
Miss Van Harlem he scarcely said three words.
In fact, he said exactly three words, uttered as
Miss Margaret's silken skirts swung too near a pot
of varnish.   They were " Look out, miss!" and
at the same second, Tommy (who was in advance,
with really no call to know of the danger), turned

on his heel and whisked the skirts away, turning
back to pick up the sentence he had dropped.

Tommy told Harry that Miss Van Harlem was
a very handsome lady, but haughty-looking.
Then he talked for half an hour about the clever-
ness of Mrs. Carriswood.

"I am inclined to think Tommy will rise."
(Mrs. Carriswood was describing the interview to
her cousin, the next day.) "What do you think
he said to me last of all? 'How,' said he, ' does
a man, a gentleman '—it had a touch of the
pathetic, don't you know, the little hesitation he
made on the word—' how does he show his gratitude to a lady who has done him a great service?' 'Young or old?' I said. ' Oh, a married
lady,' he said, ' very much admired, who has been
everywhere.' Wasn't that clever of him? I told
him that a man usually sent a few flowers. You
saw the basket to-day—evidently regardless of
expense. And fancy, there was a card, a card
with a gilt edge and his name written on it."

"The card was his mother's. She has visiting
cards, now, and pays visits once a year in a livery
carriage. Poor Mrs. Fitzmaurice, she is always so
scared ; and she is such a good soul ! Tommy is
very good to her."

8

"How about the father? Does he still keep that 'nice' saloon?"

"Yes; but he talks of retiring. They are not

"She has visiting cards, now, and pays visits once a year."

poor at all, and Tommy is their only child; the others died. It is hard on the old man to retire, for he isn't so very old in fact, but if he once is convinced that his calling stands in the way of Tommy's career, he won't hesitate a second."

"Poor people," said Mrs. Carriswood; "do you know, Grace, I can see Tommy's future; he will grow to be a boss, a political boss. He will become rich by keeping your streets always being cleaned—which means never clean—and giving you the worst fire department and police to be obtained for money; and, by and by, a grateful machine will make him mayor, or send him to the Legislature, very likely to Congress, where he will misrepresent the honest State of Iowa. Then he will bloom out in a social way, and marry a gentlewoman, and they will snub the old people who are so proud of him."

"Well, we shall see," said Mrs. Lossing; "I think better things of Tommy. So does Harry."

Part of the prophecy was to be speedily fulfilled. Two years later, the Honorable Thomas Fitzmaurice was elected mayor of his city, elected by the reform party, on account of his eminent services—and because he was the only man in sight who had the ghost of a chance of winning. Harry's version was: "Tommy jests at his new principles, but that is simply because he doesn't comprehend what they are. He laughs

at reform in the abstract; but every concrete,
practical reform he is as anxious as I or anybody
to bring about. And he will get them here,
too."

He was as good as his word; he gave the city
an admirable administration, with neither fear nor
favor. Some of the " boys " still clung to him;
these, according to Harry, were the better
" boys," who had the seeds of good in them and
only needed opportunity and a leader. Tommy
did not flag in zeal; rather, as the time went on
and he soared out of the criminal courts into big
civil cases involving property, he grew up to the
level of his admirers' praises. " Tommy," wrote
Mr. Lossing, presently, " is beginning to take
himself seriously. He has been told so often
that he is a young lion of reform, that he be-
gins to study the rôle in dead earnest. I don't
talk this way to Harry, who believes in him and
is training him for the representative for our dis-
trict. What harm? Verily, his is the faith that
will move mountains. Besides, Tommy is now
rich; he must be worth a hundred thousand
dollars, which makes a man of wealth in these
parts. It is time for him to be respectable."

Notwithstanding this preparation, Mrs. Carris-

wood (then giving Washington the benefit of
her doubts of climate) was surprised one day to
receive a perfectly correct visiting card whereon
was engraved, " Mr. Thomas Sackville Fitzmaurice, M.C."

The young lady who was with her lifted her
brilliant hazel eyes and half smiled. " Is it the
droll young man we met once at Mrs. Lossing's?
Pray see him, Aunt Margaret," said Miss Van
Harlem.

Mrs. Carriswood shrugged her shoulders and
ordered the man to show him up.

There entered, in the wake of the butler, a dis-
tinguished-looking personage who held out his
hand with a perfect copy of the bow that she saw
forty times a day. " He is taking himself very
seriously," she sighed ; " he is precisely like anybody else!" And she felt her interest snuffed
out by Tommy's correctness. But, directly, she
changed her mind; the unfailing charm of his
race asserted itself in Tommy; she decided that
he was a delightful, original young man, and in
ten minutes they were talking in the same odd
confidence that had always marked their relation.

" How perfectly you are gotten up! Are you
inside, now? "

"Ah, do you remember that?" said he; "that's awfully good of you. Which is so fortunate as to please you, my clothes or my deportment?"

"Both. They are very good. Where did you get them, Tommy? I shall take the privilege of my age and call you Tommy."

"Thank you. The clothes? Oh, I asked Harry for the proper thing, and he recommended a tailor. I think Harry gave me the manners, too."

"And your new principles?" She could not resist this little fling.

"I owe a great deal in that way to Harry, also," answered he, with gravity.

Gone were the days of sarcastic ridicule, of visionary politics. Tommy talked of the civil service in the tone of Harry himself. He was actually eloquent.

"Why, Aunt Margaret, he is a remarkable young man," exclaimed Miss Van Harlem; "his honesty and enthusiasm are refreshing in this pessimist place. I hope he will come again. Did you notice what lovely eyes he has?"

Before long it was not pure good-nature that caused Mrs. Carriswood to ask Fitzmaurice to her

house. He was known as a rising young man. One met him at the best houses; yet he was a prodigious worker, and had made his mark in committees, before the celebrated speech that sent him into all the newspaper columns, or that stubborn and infinitely versatile fight against odds which inspired the artist of *Puck*.

Tommy bore the cartoon to Mrs. Carriswood, beaming. She had not seen that light in his face since the memorable June afternoon in the Opera-house. He sent the paper to his mother, who vowed the picture "did not favor Tommy at all, at all. Sure Tommy never had such a red nose!" The old man, however, went to his ex-saloon, and sat in state all the morning, showing Tommy's funny picture.

It was about this time that Mrs. Carriswood observed something that took her breath away: Tommy Fitzmaurice had the presumption to be attentive to my lady's goddaughter, Miss Van Harlem. Nor was this the worst; there were indications that Miss Van Harlem, who had re-fused the noble names and titles of two or three continental nobles, and the noble name unaccom-panied by a title of the younger son of an English earl, without mentioning the half-dozen "nice"

American claimants—Miss Van Harlem was not angry.

The day this staggering blow fell on her, Mrs. Carriswood was in her dressing-room, peacefully watching Derry unpack a box from Paris, in anticipation of a state dinner. And Miss Van Harlem, in a bewitching wrapper, sat on the lounge and admired. Upon this scene of feminine peace and happiness enter the Destroyer, in the shape of a note from Tommy Fitzmaurice! Were they going on Beatoun's little excursion to Alexandria? If they were, he would move heaven and earth to put off a committee meeting, in order to join them. By the way, he was to get the floor for his speech that afternoon. Wouldn't Mrs. Carriswood come to inspire him? Perhaps Miss Van Harlem would not be bored by a little of it.

It was a well-worded note; as Mrs. Carriswood read it she realized for the first time how completely Tommy was acclimated in society. She remembered his plaint years ago, and his awe of " oil paintings " and " people of culture ; " and she laughed half-sadly as she passed the note over to Miss Van Harlem.

" I presume it is the Alexandria excursion that

the Beatouns were talking about yesterday," she said, languidly. " He wants to show that young Irishman that we have a mild flavor of antiquity, ourselves. We are to see Alexandria and have a real old Virginian dinner, including one of the famous Beatoun hams and some of the '69 Château Yquem and the sacred '47 port. I suppose he will have the four-in-hand buckboard. ' A small party '—that will mean the Honorable Basil Sackville, Mrs. Beatoun, Lilly Denning, probably one of the Cabinet girls, Colonel Turner, and that young Russian Beatoun is so fond of, Tommy Fitzmaurice——"

" Why do you always call Mr. Fitzmaurice Tommy ? "—this interruption comes with a slight rise of color from young Margaret.

" Everybody calls him Tommy in his own town ; a politician as popular as he with the boys is naturally Tommy or Jerry or Billy. They slap him on the back or sit with an arm around his neck and concoct the ways to rule us."

" I don't think anyone slaps Mr. Fitzmaurice on the back and calls him Tommy, *now*," says Margaret, with a little access of dignity.

" I dare say his poor old father and mother

don't venture on that liberty; I wish you had
seen them——"

"He has told me about them," says Margaret.

And Mrs. Carriswood's dismay was such that
for a second she simply gasped. Were things
so far along that such confessions were made?
Tommy must be very confident to venture; it
was shrewd, very shrewd, to forestall Mrs. Carriswood's sure revelations—oh, Tommy was not
a politician for nothing!

"Besides," Margaret went on, with the same
note of repressed feeling in her voice, "his is a
good family, if they have decayed; his ancestor
was Lord Fitzmaurice in King James's time."

"She takes *him* seriously too!" thought Mrs.
Carriswood, with inexpressible consternation;
"what *shall* I say to her mother?"

Strange to say, perhaps, considering that she
was so frankly a woman of the world, her stub-
bornest objection to Tommy was not an objection
of expediency. She had insensibly grown to take
his success for granted, like the rest of the Washington world; he would be a governor, a senator,
he might be—anything! And he was perfectly
presentable, now; no, it would be on the whole
an investment in the future that would pay well

enough; his parents would be awkward, but they were old people, not likely to be too much *en évidence*.

Mrs. Carriswood, while not overjoyed, would not feel crushed by such a match, but she did view what she regarded as Tommy's moral instability, with a dubious and fearful eye. He was earnest enough for his new principles now; but what warrant was there of his sincerity? Margaret and her mother were high-minded women. It was the gallant knight of her party and her political faith that the girl admired, the valiant fight, not the triumph! No mere soldier of fortune, no matter how successful or how brilliant, could win her; if Tommy were the mercenary, not the knight, no worldly glory could compensate his wife.

Wherefore, after a bad quarter of an hour reflecting on these things, Mrs. Carriswood went to the Capitol, resolved to take her goddaughter away. She would not withdraw her acceptance of the Beatouns' invitation, no; let the Iowa congressman have every opportunity to display his social shortcomings in contrast with the accomplished Russian, and Jack Turner, the most elegant man in the army; the next day would be

time enough for a telegram and a sudden flitting.
Yet in the midst of her plans for Tommy's dis-
comfiture she was assailed by a queer regret and
reluctance.   Tommy's fascination had affected
even a professional critic of life ; he had been so
amusing, so willing, so trusting, so useful, that
her chill interest had warmed into liking.   She
felt a moving of the heart as the handsome black
head arose, and the first notes of that resonant,
thrilling voice swelled above the din on the floor.

It was the day of his great speech, the speech
that made him, it was said.

As Mrs. Carriswood sank back, turning a little
in an instinctive effort to repulse her own sympathy, she was aware of the presence near her of
an elderly man and woman.   The old man wore a
shining silk hat and shining new black clothes.
His expansive shirt-bosom was very white, but
not glossy, and rumpled in places ; and his collar
was of the spiked and antique pattern known as
a " dickey."   His wrinkled, red face was edged
by a white fringe of whisker.   He wore large
gold-bowed spectacles, and his jaws worked in-
cessantly.

The woman was a little, mild, wrinkled creature, with an anxious blue eye and snowy hair,

smoothed down over her ears, under her fine
bonnet. She was richly dressed, but her silks
and velvets ill suited the season. Had she seen
them anywhere else, Mrs. Carriswood might not
have recognized them; but there, with Tommy
before them, both of them feverishly absorbed in
Tommy, she recognized them at a glance. She
had a twinge of pity, watching the old faces pale
and kindle. With the first rustle of applause,
she saw the old father slip his hand into the old
mother's. They sat well behind a pillar; and
however excited they became, they never so lost
themselves as to lean in front of their shield.
This, also, she noticed. The speech over, the
woman wiped her eyes. The old man joined in
the tumult of applause that swept over the gal-
leries, but the old woman pulled his arm, evidently feeling that it was not decent for them to
applaud. She sat rigid, with red cheeks and her
eyes brimming; he was swaying and clapping and
laughing in a roar of delight. But it was he that
drew her away, finally, while she fain would have
lingered to look at Tommy receiving congratulations below.

"Poor things," said Mrs. Carriswood, "I do
believe they haven't let him know that they are

here." And she remembered how she had pitied
them for this very possibility of humiliation years
before. But she did not pursue the adventure,
and some obscure motive prevented her speaking
of it to Miss Van Harlem.

Did Tommy's parents tell Tommy? If they
did, Tommy made no sign. The morning found
him with the others, in a beautiful white flannel
suit, with a silk shirt and a red silk sash, looking
handsomer than any man of the party. He took
the congratulations of the company modestly.
Either he was not much puffed up, or he had the
art of concealment.

They saw Alexandria in a conscientious fashion, for the benefit of the guest of the day. He
was a modest young fellow with a nose rather too
large for his face, a long upper lip, and frank blue
eyes. He made himself agreeable to one of the
Cabinet girls, on the front seat, while Tommy,
just behind him, had Miss Van Harlem and bliss
for his portion.

The old streets, the toppling roofs, the musty
warehouses, the uneven pavement, all pleased the
young creatures out in the sunshine. They made
merry over the ancient ball-room, where Washington had asked a far-away ancestress of Beatoun to

dance; and they decorously walked through the
old church.

It happened in the church. Mrs. Carriswood
was behind the others; so she saw them come in,
the same little old couple of the Capitol.

In the chancel, Beatoun was explaining; beside Beatoun shone a curly black head that they
knew.

Mrs. Carriswood sat in one of the high old
pews. Through a crack she could look into the
next pew; and there they stood. She heard the
old man: "Whist, Molly, let's be getting out of
this! *He* is here with all his grand friends.
Don't let us be interrupting him."

The old woman's voice was so like Tommy's
that it made Mrs. Carriswood start. Very softly
she spoke: " I only want to look at him a minute, Pat, jest a minute. I ain't seen him for so
long."

" And is it any longer for you than for me ? "
retorted the husband. " Ye know what ye promised if I'd be taking you here, unbeknownst.
Don't look his way! Look like ye was a stranger
to him. Don't let us be mortifying him wid our
country ways. Like as not 'tis the prisidint,
himself, he is colloguein' wid, this blessed min-

9

ute. Shtep back and be a stranger to him,
woman !"

A stranger to him, his own mother! But she
stepped back ; she turned her patient face. Then
—Tommy saw her.

A wave of red flushed all over his face. He
took two steps down the aisle, and caught the
little figure in his arms.

"Why, mother?" he cried, "why, mother,
where did you drop from?"

And before Mrs. Carriswood could speak she
saw him step back and push young Sackville forward, crying, "This is my father, this is the boy
that knew your grandmother."

He did it so easily ; he was so entirely unaf-
fected, so perfectly unconscious, that there was
nothing at all embarrassing for anyone. Even the
Cabinet girl, with a grandmother in very humble
life, who must be kept in the background, could
not feel disconcerted.

For this happy result Mrs. Carriswood owns a
share of the credit. She advanced on the first
pause, and claimed acquaintanceship with the
Fitzmaurices. The story of their last meeting
and Tommy's first triumph in oratory came, of
course ; the famous horseshoe received due men-

tion; and Tommy described with much humor his terror of the stage. From the speech to its most effective passage was a natural transition; equally natural the transition to Tommy's grandmother, the Irish famine, and the benevolence of Lady Sackville.

Everybody was interested, and it was Sackville himself, who brought the Fitzmaurices' noble ancestors, the apocryphal Viscounts Fitzmaurice of King James's creation, on to the carpet.

He was entirely serious. "My grandmother told me of your great-grandfather, Lord Fitzmaurice; she saw him ride to hounds once, when she was a little girl. They say he was the boldest rider in Ireland, and a renowned duellist too. King James gave the title to his grandfather, didn't he? and the countryside kept it, if it was given rather too late in the day to be useful. I am glad you have restored the family fortunes, Mr. Fitzmaurice."

The Cabinet girl looked on Tommy with respect, and Miss Van Harlem blushed like an angel.

"All is lost," said Mrs. Carriswood to herself; yet she smiled. Going home, she found a word for Tommy's ear. The old Virginian dinner had

been most successful. The Fitzmaurices (who
had been almost forced into the banquet by Beatoun's imperious hospitality) were not a wet blan-
ket in the least. Patrick Fitzmaurice, brogue and
all, was an Irish gentleman without a flaw. He
blossomed out into a modest wag ; and told two
or three comic stories as acceptably as he was
used to tell them to a very different circle—only,
carrying a fresher flavor of wit to this circle, perhaps, it enjoyed them more. Mrs. Fitzmaurice
looked scared and ate almost nothing, with the
greatest propriety, and her fork in her left hand.
Yet even she thawed under Miss Van Harlem's
attentions and gentle Mrs. Beatoun's tact, and
the winning ways of the last Beatoun baby. She
took this absent cherub to her heart with such
undissembled warmth that its mother ever since
has called her "a sweet, funny little old lady."

They were both (Patrick and his wife) quite
unassuming and retiring, and no urging could dis-
suade them from parting with the company at the
tavern door.

"My word, Tommy, your mother and I can git
home by ourselves," whispered honest Patrick ;
" we've not exceeded—if the wines *were* good.   I
never exceeded in my life, God take the glory !"

But he embraced Tommy so affectionately in parting that I confess Mrs. Carriswood had suspicions. Yet, surely, it is more likely that his brain was—let us not say *turned*, but just a wee bit *tilted*, by the joy and triumph of the occasion rather than by Beatoun's port or champagne.

But Mrs. Carriswood's word had nothing to do with Tommy's parents, ostensibly, though, in truth, it had everything to do. She said: "Will you dine with us to-morrow, quite *en famille*, Thomas?"

"I ought to tell you, I suppose, that I find your house a pretty dangerous paradise, Mrs. Carriswood," says Tommy.

"And I find you a most dangerous angel, Thomas; but—you see I ask you!"

"Thank you," answers Tommy, in a different tone; "you've always been an angel to me. What I owe to you and Harry Lossing—well, I can't talk about it. But see here, Mrs. Carriswood, you always have called me Tommy; now you say Thomas; why this state?"

"I think you have won your brevet, Thomas."

He looked puzzled, and she liked him the better that he should not make enough of his conduct to understand her; but, though she

has called him Tommy often since, he keeps
the brevet in her thoughts.   In fact, Mrs. Carriswood is beginning to take the Honorable Thomas
Fitzmaurice and his place in the world seriously,
herself.

MOTHER EMERITUS

THE Louders lived on the second floor, at the head of the stairs, in the Lossing Building. There is a restaurant to the right ; and a new doctor, every six months, who is every kind of a healer except " regular," keeps the permanent boarders in gossip, to the left ; two or three dressmakers, a dentist, and a diamond merchant up-stairs, one flight ; and half a dozen families and a dozen single tenants higher—so you see the Louders had plenty of neighbors. In fact, the multitude of the neighbors is one cause of my story.

Tilly Louder came home from the Lossing factory (where she is a typewriter) one February afternoon. As she turned the corner, she was face to the river, which is not so full of shipping in winter that one cannot see the steel-blue glint of the water. Back of her the brick paved street climbed the hill, under a shapeless arch of trees. The remorseless pencil of a railway has drawn

black lines at the foot of the hill; and, all day
and all night, slender red bars rise and sink in
their black sockets, to the accompaniment of the
outcry of tortured steam. All day, if not all
night, the crooked pole slips up and down the
trolley wire, as the yellow cars rattle, and flash,
and clang a spiteful little bell, that sounds like a
soprano bark, over the crossings.

It is customary in the Lossing Building to say,
"We are so handy to the cars." The street is a
handsome street, not free from dingy old brick
boxes of stores below the railway, but fast replac-
ing them with fairer structures. The Lossing
Building has the wide arches, the recessed doors,
the balconies and the colonnades of modern business architecture. The occupants are very proud
of the balconies, in particular; and, summer days,
these will be a mass of greenery and bright tints.
To-day, it was so warm, February day though it
was, that some of the potted plants were sunning
themselves outside the windows.

Tilly could see them if she craned her neck.
There were some bouvardias and fuchsias of her
mother's among them.

"It *is* a pretty building," said Tilly; and, for
some reason, she frowned.

She was a young woman, but not a very young woman. Her figure was slim, and she looked better in loose waists than in tightly fitted gowns. She wore a dark green gown with a black jacket, and a scarlet shirt-waist underneath. Her face was long, with square chin and high cheek-bones, and thin, firm lips; yet she was comely, because of her lustrous black hair, her clear, gray eyes, and her charming, fair skin. She had another gift : everything about her was daintily neat ; at first glance one said, " Here is a person who has spent pains, if not money, on her toilet."

By this time Tilly was entering the Lossing Building. Half-way up the stairway a hand plucked her skirts. The hand belonged to a tired-faced woman in black, on whose breast glittered a little crowd of pins and threaded needles, like the insignia of an Order of Toil.

" Please excuse me, Miss Tilly," said the woman, at the same time presenting a flat package in brown paper, " but *will* you give this pattern back to your mother. I am so very much obliged. I don't know how I *would* git along without your mother, Tilly."

" I'll give the pattern to her," said Tilly, and she pursued her way.

Not very far. A stout woman and a thin
young man, with long, wavy, red hair, awaited
her on the landing. The woman held a plate of
cake which she thrust at Tilly the instant they
were on the same level, saying: "The cake was
just splendid, tell your mother; it's a lovely
recipe, and will you tell her to take this, and see
how well I succeeded?"

"And—ah—Miss Louder," said the man, as the
stout woman rustled away, "here are some *Banner of Lights;* I think she'd be interested in some
of the articles on the true principles of the inspi-
rational faith——" Tilly placed the bundle of
newspapers at the base of her load—"and—and,
I wish you'd tell your dear mother that, under
the angels, her mustard plaster really saved
my life."

"I'll tell her," said Tilly.

She had advanced a little space before a young
girl in a bright blue silk gown flung a radiant
presence between her and the door. "Oh, Miss
Tilly," she murmured, blushing, "will you just
give your mother this?—it's—it's Jim's photograph. You tell her it's *all* right : and *she* was exactly right, and *I* was wrong. She'll understand."

Tilly, with a look of resignation, accepted a

" The cake was just splendid."

stiff package done up in white tissue paper. She
had now only three steps to take : she took two,
only two, for — " Miss Tilly, *please!* " a voice
pealed around the corner, while a flushed and
breathless young woman, with a large baby toppling over her lean shoulder, staggered into view.
" My ! " she panted, " ain't it tiresome lugging a
child ! I missed the car, of course, coming home
from ma's. Oh, say, Tilly, your mother was so
good, she said she'd tend Blossom next time I
went to the doctor's, and——"

" I'll take the baby," said Tilly. She hoisted
the infant on to her own shoulder with her right
arm. " Perhaps you'll be so kind's to turn the
handle of the door," said she in a slightly caustic
tone, " as I haven't got any hands left. Please
shut it, too."

As the young mother opened the door, Tilly
entered the parlor. For a second she stood and
stared grimly about her. The furniture of the
room was old-fashioned but in the best repair.
There was a cabinet organ in one corner. A
crayon portrait of Tilly's father (killed in the
civil war) glared out of a florid gilt frame. Perhaps it was the fault of the portrait, but he had
a peevish frown. There were two other portraits

of him, large ghastly gray tintypes in oval frames
of rosewood, obscurely suggesting coffins. In
these he looked distinctly sullen. He was rep-
resented in uniform (being a lieutenant of volun-
teers), and the artist had conscientiously gilded
his buttons until, as Mrs. Louder was wont to
observe, "It most made you want to cut them
off with the scissors." There were other tintypes and a flock of photographs in the room.
What Mrs. Louder named "a throw" decorated
each framed picture and each chair. The largest
arm-chair was drawn up to a table covered with
books and magazines: in the chair sat Mrs.
Louder, reading.

At Tilly's entrance she started and turned her
head, and then one could see that the tears were
streaming down her cheeks.

"Now, *mother!*" exploded Tilly. Kicking the
door open, she marched into the bed-chamber.
An indignant sweep of one arm sent the miscel-
lany of gifts into a rocking-chair; an indignant
curve of the other landed the baby on the bed.
Tilly turned on her mother. "Now, mother,
what did you promise—*hush!* will you?" (The
latter part of the sentence a fierce "*aside*" to the
infant on the bed.) In a second Mrs. Louder's

arms were encircling him, and she was soothing
him on her broad shoulder, where I know not
how many babies have found comfort.

Jane Louder was a tall woman—tall and portly.
She had a massive repose about her, a kind of
soft dignity ; and a stranger would not guess how
tender was her heart. Deprecatingly she looked
up at her only child, standing in judgment over
her. Her eyes were fine still, though they had
sparkled and wept for more than half a century.
They were not gray, like Tilly's, but a deep violet,
with black eyelashes and eyebrows. Black, once,
had been the hair under the widow's cap, now
streaked with silver ; but Jane Louder's skin was
fresh and daintily tinted like her daughter's, for
all its fine wrinkles. Her voice when she spoke
was mellow and slow, with a nervous vibration
of apology. " Never mind, dear," she said, " I
was just reading 'bout the Russians."

" I *knew* it ! You promised me you wouldn't
cry about the Russians any more."

" I know, Tilly, but Alma Brown lent this to
me, herself. There's a beautiful article in it about
' The Horrors of Hunger.' It would make your
heart ache ! I wish you would read it, Tilly."

" No, thank you. I don't care to have my

heart ache. I'm not going to read any more
horrors about the Russians, or hear them either,
if I can help it. I have to write Mr. Lossing's
letters about them, and that's enough. I've
given all I can afford, and you've given more
than you can afford ; and I helped get up the
subscription at the shops. I've done all I could ;
and now I ain't going to have my feelings har-
rowed up any more, when it won't do me nor the
Russians a mite of good."

"But I cayn't *help* it, Tilly. I cayn't take any
comfort in my meals, thinking of that awful black
bread the poor children starve rather than eat ;
and, Tilly, they ain't so dirty as some folks think !
I read in a magazine how they have *got* to bathe
twice a week by their religion ; and there's a
bath-house in every village. Tilly, do you know
how much money they've raised here ?"

"Over three thousand. This town is the
greatest town for giving—give to the cholera
down South, give to Johnstown, give to Grinnell,
give to cyclones, give to fires. *The Freeman* always starts up a subscription, and Mr. Bayard
runs the thing, and Mr. Lossing always gives.
Mother, I tell you *he* makes them hustle when
he takes hold. He's the chairman here, and he

has township chairmen appointed for every township. He's so popular they start in to oblige
him, and then, someway, he makes them all interested. I must tell you of a funny letter he
had to-day from a Captain Ferguson, out at
Baxter. He's a rich farmer with lots of influence
and a great worker, Mr. Lossing says. But this
is 'most word for word what he wrote: 'Dear
Sir: I am sorry for the Russians, but my wife is
down with the la grippe, and I can't get a hired
girl; so I have to stay with her. If you'll get
me a hired girl, I'll get you a lot of money for
the Russians.' "

"Did he git a girl? I mean Mr. Lossing."

"No, ma'am. He said he'd try if it was the
city, but it was easier finding gold-mines than
girls that would go into the country. See here,
I'm forgetting your presents. Mother, you look
real dragged and—queer ! "

"It's nothing; jist a thought kinder struck me
'bout—'bout that girl."

Tilly was sorting out the parcels and explaining them; at the end of her task her mind harked
back to an old grievance. "Mother," said she,
"I've been thinking for a long time, and I've
made up my mind."

"Yes, dearie." Mrs. Louder's eyes grew troubled. She knew something of the quality of Tilly's mind, which resembled her father's in a peculiar immobility. Once let her decision run into any mould (be it whatsoever it might), and let it stiffen, there was no chance, any more than with other iron things, of its bending.

"Positively I could hardly get up the stairs to-day," said Tilly—she was putting her jacket and hat away in her orderly fashion ; of necessity her back was to Mrs. Louder—"there was such a raft of people wanting to send stuff and messages to you. You are just working yourself to death ; and, mother, I am convinced we have *got to move !* "

Mrs. Louder dropped into a chair and gasped. The baby, who had fallen asleep, stirred uneasily. It was not a pretty child ; its face was heavy, its little cheeks were roughened by the wind, its lower lip sagged, its chin creased into the semblance of a fat old man's. But Jane Louder gazed down on it with infinite compassion. She stroked its head as she spoke.

"Tilly," said she, "I've been in this block, Mrs. Carleton and me, ever since it was built ; and, some way, between us we've managed to keep the run of all the folks in it ; at least when

10

they were in any trouble. We've worked together like sisters. She's 'Piscopal, and I guess
I'm Unitarian; but never a word between us.
We tended the Willardses through diphtheria
and the Hopkinses through small-pox, and we
steamed and fumigated the rooms together. It
was her first found out the Dillses were letting
that twelve-year-old child run the gasoline stove,
and she threatened to tell Mr. Lossing, and they
begged off; and when it exploded we put it out
together, with flour out of her flour-barrel, for
the poor, shiftless things hadn't half a sack full
of their own; and her and me, we took half the
care of that little neglected Ellis baby that was
always sitting down in the sticky fly-paper, poor
innocent child. He's took the valedictory at the
High School, Tilly, now. No, Tilly, I couldn't
bring myself to leave this building, where I've
married them, and buried them, and born them,
you may say, being with so many of their
mothers; I feel like they was all my children.
Don't *ask* me."

Tilly's head went upward and backward with a
little dilatation of the nostrils. " Now, mother,"
said she in a voice of determined gentleness,
" just listen to me. Would I ask you to do any-

"We put it out together with flour out of her flour-barrel."

thing that wouldn't be for your happiness? I
have found a real pretty house up on Fifteenth
Street; and we'll keep house together, just as
cosey; and have a woman come to wash and iron
and scrub, so it won't be a bit hard; and be right
on the street-cars; and you won't have to drudge
helping Mrs. Carleton extra times with her restaurant."

"But, Tilly," eagerly interrupted Mrs. Louder,
"you know I dearly love to cook, and she *pays*
me. I couldn't feel right to take any of the
pension money, or the little property your father
left me, away from the house expenses; but what
I earn myself, it is *such* a comfort to give away
out of *that*."

Tilly ran over and kissed the agitated face.
"You dear, generous mother!" cried she, "*I'll*
give you all the money you want to spend or
give. I got another rise in my salary of five a
month. Don't you worry."

"You ain't thinking of doing anything right
away, Tilly?"

"Don't you think it's best done and over with,
after we've decided, mother? You have worked
so hard all your life I want to give you some ease
and peace now."

" But, Tilly, I love to work ; I wouldn't be happy to do nothing, and I'd get so fleshy ! "

Tilly only laughed. She did not crave the show of authority. Let her but have her own way, she would never flaunt her victories. She was imperious, but she was not arrogant. For months she had been pondering how to give her mother an easier life ; and she set the table for supper, in a filial glow of satisfaction, never dreaming that her mother, in the kitchen, was keeping her head turned from the stove lest she should cry into the fried ham and stewed potatoes. But, at a sudden thought, Jane Louder laid her big spoon down to wipe her eyes.

" Here you are, Jane Louder "—thus she addressed herself—" mourning and grieving to leave your friends and be laid aside for a useless old woman, and jist be taken care of, and you clean forgetting the chance the Lord gives you to help more'n you ever helped in your life ! For shame ! "

A smile of exaltation, of lofty resolution, erased the worry lines on her face. " Why, it might be to save twenty lives," said she ; but in the very speaking of the words a sharp pain wrenched her heart again, and she caught up

the baby from the floor, where he sat in a wall
of chairs, and sobbed over him: "Oh, how can I
go away when I got to go for good so soon? I
want every minnit!"

She never thought of disputing Tilly's wishes.
"It's only fair," said Jane. "She's lived here all
these years to please me, and now I ought to be
willing to go to please her."

Neither did she for a moment hope to change
Tilly's determination. "She was the settest baby
ever was," thought poor Jane, tossing on her pillow, in the night watches, "and it's grown with
every inch of her!"

But in the morning she surprised her daughter.
"Tilly," said she at the breakfast-table, "Tilly,
I got something I must do, and I don't want you
to oppose me."

"Good gracious, ma!" said Tilly; "as if I ever
opposed you!"

"You know how bad I have been feeling about
the poor Russians——"

"Well?"

"And how I've wished and wished I could do
something—something to *count?* I never could,
Tilly, because I ain't got the money or the intel-
lect; but s'posing I could do it for somebody

else, like this Captain Ferguson who could do so much if he just could get a hired girl to take care of his wife. Well, I do know how to cook and to keep a house neat and to do for the sick——"

Tilly could restrain herself no longer; her voice rose to a shout of dismay—"Mother Louder, you *ain't* thinking of going to be the Ferguson's *hired girl!*"

" Not their hired girl, Tilly; just their help, so as he can work for those poor starving creatures." Jane strangled a sob in her throat. Tilly, in a kind of stupor of bewilderment, frowned at her plate. Then her clouded face cleared. If Mrs. Louder had surprised her daughter, her daughter repaid the surprise. "Well, if you feel that way, mother," said she, " I won't say a word; and I'll ask Mr. Lossing to explain to the Fergusons and fix everything. He will."

" You're real good, Tilly."

"And while you're gone I guess it will be a good plan to move and git settled——"

For some reason Tilly's throat felt dry, she lifted her cup. She did not intend to look across the table, but her eyes escaped her. She set the coffee down untasted. The clock was slow, she muttered; and she left the room.

Jane Louder remained in her place, with the same pale face, staring at the table-cloth.

"It don't seem like I *could* go, now," she thought dully to herself; "the time's so awful short, I don't s'pose Maria Carleton can git up to see me more'n once or twice a month, busy as she is! I got so to depend on seeing her every day. A sister couldn't be kinder! I don't see how I am going to bear it. And to go away, before-hand——"

For a long while she sat, her face hardly changing. At last, when she did push her chair away, her lips were tightly closed. She spoke to the little pile of books lying on the table in the corner. "I cayn't—these are my own and you are strangers!" She walked across the room to take up the same magazine which Tilly had found her reading the day before. When she began reading she looked stern—poor Jane, she was steeling her heart—but in a little while she was sniffing and blowing her nose. With a groan she flung the book aside. "It's no use, I would feel like a murderer if I don't go!" said she.

She did go. Harry Lossing made all the arrangements. Tilly was satisfied. But, then, Tilly had not heard Harry's remark to his mother: "Alma says Miss Louder is trying to make the old lady move against her will. I dare say it would be better to give the young woman a chance to miss her mother and take a little quiet think."

Tilly saw her mother off on the train to Baxter, the Fergusons' station. Being a provident, far-sighted, and also inexperienced traveller, she had allowed a full half-hour for preliminary passages at arms with the railway officials; and, as the train happened to be an hour late, she found herself with time to spare, even after she had exhausted the catalogue of possible deceptions and catastrophes by rail. During the silence that followed her last warning, she sat mentally keeping tally on her fingers. " Confidence men " —Tilly began with the thumb—" Never give anybody her check. Never lend anybody money. Never write her name to anything. Don't get out till conductor tells her. In case of accident, telegraph me, and keep in the middle of the car, off the trucks. Not take care of anybody's baby while she goes off for a minute. Not take care of babies at all. Or children. Not talk to strangers —good gracious !"

Tilly felt a movement of impatience; there,

after all her cautions, there was her mother helping an old woman, an utterly strange old woman,
to pile a bird-cage on a bandbox surmounting a
bag. The old woman was clad in a black alpaca
frock, made with the voluminous draperies of
years ago, but with the uncreased folds and the
brilliant gloss of a new gown. She wore a bonnet of a singular shape, unknown to fashion, but
made out of good velvet. Beneath the bonnet
(which was large) appeared a little, round, agitated old face, with bobbing white curls and white
teeth set a little apart in the mouth, a defect that
brought a kind of palpitating frankness into the
expression.

"Now, who *has* mother picked up now?"
thought Tilly. "Well, praise be, she hasn't a
baby, anyhow!"

She could hear the talk between the two; for
the old woman being deaf, Mrs. Louder elevated
her voice, and the old woman, herself, spoke in a
high, thin pipe that somehow reminded Tilly of
a lost lamb.

"That's just so," said Mrs. Louder, "a body
cayn't help worrying over a sick child, especially if
they're away from you."

"Solon and Minnie wouldn't tell me," bleated

the other woman, "they knew I'd worry. Kinder
hurt me they should keep things from me; but
they hate to have me upset. They are awful
good children. But I suspicioned something
when Alonzo kept writing. Minnie, she wouldn't
tell me, but I pinned her down and it come out,
Eliza had the grip bad. And, then, nothing
would do but I must go to her—why, Mrs.
Louder, she's my child! But they wouldn't hark
to it. 'Fraid to have me travel alone——"

"I guess they take awful good care of you,"
said Mrs. Louder; and she sighed.

"Yes, ma'am, awful." She, too, sighed.

As she talked her eyes were darting about the
room, eagerly fixed on every new arrival.

"Are you expecting anyone, Mrs. Higbee?"
said Jane. They seemed, at least, to know each
other by name, thought Tilly; it was amazing the
number of people mother did know!

"No," said Mrs. Higbee, "I—I—fact is, I'm
kinder frightened. I—fact is, Mrs. Louder, I
guess I'll tell you, though I don't know you very
well; but I've known about you so long—I run
away and didn't tell 'em. I just couldn't stay
way from Liza. And I took the bird—for the
children; and it's my bird, and I was 'fraid Minnie

would forget to feed it and it would be lonesome.
My children are awful kind good children, but
they don't understand. And if Solon sees me
he will want me to go back. I know I'm dretful
foolish; and Solon and Minnie will make me see
I am. There won't be no good reason for me to
go, and I'll have to stay; and I feel as if I should
fly—Oh, massy sakes! there's Solon coming down
the street——"

She ran a few steps in half a dozen ways, then
fluttered back to her bag and her cage.

"Well," said Mrs. Louder, drawing herself up
to her full height, "you *shall* go if you want to."

"Solon will find me, he'll know the bird-cage!
Oh, dear! Oh, dear!"

Then a most unexpected helper stepped upon
the stage. What is the mysterious instinct of
rebellion to authority that, nine cases out of ten,
sends us to the aid of a fugitive? Tilly, the
unconscious despot of her own mother, promptly
aided and abetted Solon's rebel mother in her
flight.

"Not if *I* carry it," said she, snatching up the
bird-cage; "run inside that den where they sell
refreshments; he'll see *me* and go somewhere
else."

It fell out precisely as she planned.   They heard Solon demanding a lady with a bird-cage of the agent ; they heard the agent's reply, given with official indifference, " There she is, inside." Directly, Solon, a small man with an anxious mien, ran into the waiting-room, flung a glance of disappointment at Tilly, and ran out again.

Tilly went to her client.   " Did he look like he was anxious ? " was the mother's greeting.   " Oh, I just know he and Minnie will be hunting me everywhere.   Maybe I had better go home, 'stead of to Baxter."

" No, you hadn't," said Tilly, with decision. " Mother's going to Baxter, too, and if you like, minnit you're safely off, I'll go tell your folks."

" You're real kind, I'd be ever so much obliged. And you don't mind your ma travelling alone ? ain't that nice for her ! "   She seemed much cheered by the prospect of company and warmed into confidences.

" I am kinder lonesome, sometimes, that's a fact," said she, " and I kinder wish I lived in a block or a flat like your ma.   You see, Minnie teaches in the public school and she's away all day, and she don't like to have me make company of the hired girl, though she's a real nice girl.

And there ain't nothing for me to do, and I feel like I wasn't no use any more in the world. I remember that's what our old minister in Ohio said once. He was a real nice old man; and they *had* thought everything of him in the parish; but he got old and his sermons were long; and so they got a young man for assistant; and they made *him* a *pastor americus*, they called it—some sort of Latin. Folks did say the young feller was stuck up and snubbed the old man; anyhow, he never preached after young Lisbon come; and only made the first prayers. But when the old folks would ask him to preach some of the old sermons they had liked, he only would say, ' No, friends, I know more about my sermons, now.' He didn't live very long, and I always kinder fancied being a *americus* killed him. And some days I git to feeling like I was a kinder *americus* myself."

"That ain't fair to your children," said Tilly; "you ought to let them know how you feel. Then they'd act different."

"Oh, I don't know, I don't know. You see, miss, they're so sure they know better'n me. Say, Mrs. Louder, be you going to visit relatives in Baxter?"

" No, ma'am, I'm going to take care of a sick
lady," said Jane, " it's kinder queer.   Her name's
Ferguson, her——"

" For the land's sake !" screamed Mrs. Higbee,
" why, that's my 'Liza !"   She was in a flutter of
surprise and delight, and so absorbed was Tilly in
getting her and her unwieldy luggage into the car,
that Jane's daughter forgot to kiss her mother
good-by.

" Put your arm in *quick*," she yelled, as Jane
essayed to kiss her hand through the window ;
" don't *ever* put your arm or your head out of a
train ! "—the train moved away—" I do hope she'll
remember what I told her, and not lend anybody
money, or come home lugging somebody else's
baby ! "

With such reflections, and an ugly sensation of
loneliness creeping over her, Tilly went to assure
Miss Minnie Higbee of her mother's safety.   She
described her reception to Harry Lossing and
Alma, later.   " She really seemed kinder mad at
me," says Tilly, " seemed to think I was interfer-
ing somehow.   And she hadn't any business to
feel that way, for *she* didn't know how I'd fooled
her brother with that bird-cage.   I guess the poor
old lady daren't call her soul her own.   I'd hate

to have my mother that way—so 'fraid of me. *My* mother shall go where she pleases, and stay where she pleases, and *do* as she pleases."

"That makes me think," says Alma, "I heard you were going to move."

"Yes, we are. Mother is working too hard. She knows everybody in the building, and they call on her all the time; and I think the easiest way out is just to move."

Alma and Mr. Lossing exchanged glances. There is an Arabian legend of an angel whose trade it is to decipher the language of faces. This angel must have perceived that Alma's eyes said, with the courage of a second in a duel, "Go on, now is the time!" and that Harry's answered, with masculine pusillanimity, "I don't like to!"

But he spoke. "Very likely your mother does sometimes work too hard," said he. "But don't you think it would be harder for her not to work? Why, she must have been in the building ever since my father bought it; and she's been a janitor and a fire inspector and a doctor and a ministering angel combined! That is why we never raised the rent to you when we improved the building, and raised it on the others. My father told me your mother was the best paying tenant he ever had.

11

And don't you remember how, when I used to
come with him, when I was a little boy, she used
to take me in her room while he went the rounds?
She was always doing good to everybody, the same
way. She has a heart as big as the Mississippi,
and I assure you, Miss Louder, you won't make
her happy, but miserable, if you try to dam up its
channel. She has often told me that she loved
the building and all the people in it. They all
love her. I *hope*, Miss Louder, you'll think of
those things before you decide. She is so un-
selfish that she would go in a minute if she
thought it would make you happier." The angel
aforesaid, during this speech (which Harry de-
livered with great energy and feeling), must have
had all his wits busy on Tilly's impassive features;
but he could read ardent approval, succeeded by
indignation, on Alma's countenance, at his first
glance. The indignation came when Tilly spoke.
She said : " Thank you, Mr. Lossing, you're very
kind, I'm sure "—Harry softly kicked the waste-
basket under the desk—" but I guess it's best for
us to go. I've been thinking about it for six
months, and I know it will be a hard struggle for
mother to go ; but in a little while she will be glad
she went. It's only for her sake I am doing it ;

it ain't an easy or a pleasant thing for me to do, either——" As Tilly stopped her voice was unsteady, and the rare tears shone in her eyes.

"What's best for her is the only question, of course," said Alma, helping Harry off the field.

In a few days Tilly received a long letter from her mother. Mr. Ferguson was doing wonders for the Russians; the family were all very kind to her and "nice folks" and easily pleased. ("Of *course* they're pleased with mother's cooking; what would they be made of if they weren't!" cried Tilly.) It was wonderful how much help Mrs. Higbee was about the house, and how happy it made her. Mrs. Ferguson had seemed real glad to see her, and that made her happy. And then, maybe it helped a little, her (Jane Louder's) telling Mrs. Ferguson ("accidental like") how Tilly treated her, never trying to boss her, and letting her travel alone. Perhaps, if Mrs. Ferguson kept on improving, they might let her come home next week. And the letter ended:

"I will be so glad if they do, for I want to see you so bad, dear daughter, and I want to see the old home once more before we leave. I guess the house you tell me about will be very nice and

convenient. I do thank you, dear daughter, for
being so nice and considerate about the Russians.
Give my love to Mrs. Carleton and all of them;
and if little Bobby Green hasn't missed school
since I left, give him a nickel, please; and please
give that medical student on the fifth floor—I
forget his name—the stockings I mended. They
are in the first drawer of the walnut bureau.
Good-by, my dear, good daughter.

"MOTHER, JANE M. LOUDER."

When Tilly read the letter she was surrounded
by wall-paper and carpet samples. Her eyes grew
moist before she laid it down; but she set her
mouth more firmly.

" It is an awful short time, but I've just got to
hurry and have it over before she comes," said
she.

Next week Jane returned. She was on the
train, waiting in her seat in the car, when Captain
Ferguson handed her Tilly's last letter, which had
lain in the post-office for three days.

It was very short :

" DEAR MOTHER : I shall be very glad indeed
to see you. I have a surprise which I hope will

be pleasant for you; anyhow, I truly have meant
it for your happiness.

"Your affectionate daughter,

"M. E. LOUDER."

There must have been, despite her shrewd
sense, an obtuse streak in Tilly, else she would
never have written that letter. Jane read it twice.
The paper rattled in her hands. "Tilly has moved
while I was gone," she said; "I never shall live
in the block again." She dropped her veil over
her face. She sat very quietly in her seat; but
the conductor who came for her ticket watched
her sharply, she seemed so dazed by his demand
and was so long in finding the ticket.

The train rumbled and hissed through darken-
ing cornfields, into scattered yellow lights of low
houses, into angles of white light of street-arcs
and shop-windows, into the red and blue lights
dancing before the engines in the station.

"Mother!" cried Tilly's voice.

Jane let her and Harry Lossing take all her
bundles and lift her out of the car. Whether she
spoke a word she could not tell. She did rouse
a little at the vision of the Lossing carriage glittering at the street corner; but she had not the

sense to thank Harry Lossing, who placed her in
the carriage and lifted his hat in farewell.

"What's he doing all that for, Tilly?" cried
she; "there ain't—there ain't nobody dead—
Maria Carleton——" She stared at Tilly wildly.

Tilly was oddly moved, though she tried to
speak lightly. " No, no, there ain't nothing wrong,
at all. It's because you've done so much for the
Russians—and other folks! Now, ma, I'm going
to be mysterious. You must shut your eyes and
shut your mouth until I tell you. That's a dear
ma."

It was vaguely comforting to have Tilly so
affectionate. " I'm a wicked, ungrateful woman
to be so wretched," thought Jane; " I'll never let
Tilly know how I felt."

In a surprisingly short time the carriage
stopped. " Now, ma," said Tilly.

A great blaze of light seemed all about Jane
Louder. There were the dear familiar windows of
the Lossing block.

" Come up-stairs, ma," said Tilly.

She followed like one in a dream; and like one
in a dream she was pushed into her own old parlor.
The old parlor, but not quite the old parlor; hung
with new wall-paper, shining with new paint, soft

under her feet with a new carpet, it looked to Jane
Louder like fairyland.

"Oh, Tilly," she gasped; "oh, Tilly, ain't you
moved?"

"No, nor we ain't going to move, ma—that's
the surprise! I took the money I'd saved for
moving, for the new carpet and new dishes; and
the Lossings they papered and painted. I was
so 'fraid we couldn't get done in time. Alma and
all the boarders are coming in pretty soon to welcome you, and they've all chipped in for a little
banquet at Mrs. Carleton's—why, mother, you're
crying! Mother, you didn't really think I'd
move when it made you feel so bad? I know I'm
set and stubborn, and I didn't take it well when
Mr. Lossing talked to me; but the more I thought
it over, the more I seemed to myself like that
hateful Minnie. Oh, mother, I ain't, am I? You
shall do just exactly as you like all the days of
your life!"

AN ASSISTED PROVIDENCE

IT was the Christmas turkeys that should be
held responsible. Every year the Lossings
give each head of a family in their employ, and
each lad helping to support his mother, a turkey
at Christmastide. As the business has grown, so
has the number of turkeys, until it is now well
up in the hundreds, and requires a special contract. Harry, one Christmas, some two years
ago, bought the turkeys at so good a bargain
that he felt the natural reaction in an impulse
to extravagance. In the very flood-tide of the
money-spending yearnings, he chanced to pass
Deacon Hurst's stables and to see two Saint
Bernard puppies, of elephantine size but of the
tenderest age, gambolling on the sidewalk before
the office. Deacon Hurst, I should explain, is no
more a deacon than I am ; he is a livery-stable
keeper, very honest, a keen and solemn sports-
man, and withal of a staid demeanor and a habit-
ual garb of black. Now you know as well as I
any reason for his nickname.

Deacon Hurst is fond of the dog as well as of
that noble animal the horse (he has three copies
of " Black Beauty " in his stable, which would do
an incalculable amount of good if they were ever
read!); and he usually has half a dozen dogs of
his own, with pedigrees long enough for a poor
gentlewoman in a New England village.   He told
Harry that the Saint Bernards were grandsons of
Sir Bevidere, the " finest dog of his time in the
world, sir ; " that they were perfectly marked and
very large for their age (which Harry found it
easy to believe of the young giants), and that
they were " ridiculous, sir, at the figger of two
hundred and fifty ! " (which Harry did not believe
so readily); and, after Harry had admired and
studied the dogs for the space of half an hour,
he dropped the price, in a kind of spasm of
generosity, to two hundred dollars.   Harry was
tempted to close the bargain on the spot, hot-
headed, but he decided to wait and prepare his
mother for such a large addition to the stable.

The more he dwelt on the subject the more he
longed to buy the dogs.

In fact, a time comes to every healthy man
when he wants a dog, just as a time comes when
he wants a wife ; and Harry's dog was dead.   By

"Ridiculous, sir, at the figger of two hundred and fifty!"

consequence, Harry was in the state of sensitive affection and desolation to which a promising new object makes the most moving appeal. The departed dog (Bruce by name) had been a Saint Bernard; and Deacon Hurst found one of the puppies to have so much the expression of countenance of the late Bruce that he named him Bruce on the spot—a little before Harry joined the group. Harry did not at first recognize this resemblance, but he grew to see it; and, combined with the dog's affectionate disposition, it softened his heart. By the time he told his mother he was come to quoting Hurst's adjectives as his own.

"Beauties, mother," says Harry, with sparkling eyes; "the markings are perfect—couldn't be better; and their heads are shaped just right! You can't get such watch-dogs in the world! And, for all their enormous strength, gentle as a lamb to women and children! And, mother, one of them looks like Bruce!"

"I suppose they would want to be house-dogs," says Mrs. Lossing, a little dubiously, but looking fondly at Harry's handsome face; "you know, somehow, all our dogs, no matter how properly they start in a kennel, end by being so hurt if we keep them there that they come into the house. And they are so large, it is like having a pet lion about."

" These dogs, mother, shall never put a paw in the house."

" Well, I hope just as I get fond of them they will not have the distemper and die!" said Mrs. Lossing; which speech Harry rightly took for the white flag of surrender.

That evening he went to find Hurst and clinch the bargain. As it happened, Hurst was away, driving an especially important political personage to an especially important political council. The day following was a Sunday; but, by this time, Harry was so bent upon obtaining the dogs that he had it in mind to go to Hurst's house for them in the afternoon. When Harry wants anything, from Saint Bernards to purity in politics, he wants it with an irresistible impetus! If he did wrong, his error was linked to its own punishment. But this is anticipating, if not presuming; I prefer to leave Harry Lossing's experience to paint its own moral without pushing. The event that happened next was Harry's pulling out his check-book and beginning to write a check, remarking, with a slight drooping of his eyelids,

" Best catch the deacon's generosity on the fly, or
it may make a home run!"

Then he let the pen fall on the blotter, for he
had remembered the day. After an instant's
hesitation he took a couple of hundred-dollar
bank-notes out of a drawer (I think they were
gifts for his two sisters on Christmas day, for he
is a generous brother; and most likely there
would be some small domestic joke about engravings to go with them); these he placed in the
right-hand pocket of his waistcoat. In his left-
hand waistcoat pocket were two five-dollar notes.

Harry was now arrayed for church. He was a
figure to please any woman's eye, thought his
mother, as she walked beside him, and gloried
silently in his six feet of health and muscle and
dainty cleanliness. He was in a most amiable
mood, what with the Saint Bernards and the season. As they approached the cathedral close,
Harry, not for the first time, admired the pure
Gothic lines of the cathedral, and the soft blend-
ing of grays in the stone with the warmer hues
of the brown network of Virginia creeper that
still fluttered, a remnant of the crimson adornings
of autumn. Beyond were the bare, square out-
lines of the old college, with a wooden cupola

perched on the roof, like a little hat on a fat
man, the dull-red tints of the professors' houses,
and the withered lawns and bare trees. The
turrets and balconies and arched windows of the
boys' school displayed a red background for a
troop of gray uniforms and blazing buttons ; the
boys were forming to march to church. Opposite
the boys' school stood the modest square brick
house that had served the first bishop of the
diocese during laborious years. Now it was the
dean's residence. Facing it, just as you approached the cathedral, the street curved into a
half-circle on either side, and in the centre the
granite soldier on his shaft looked over the city
that would honor him. Harry saw the tall figure
of the dean come out of his gate, the long black
skirts of his cassock fluttering under the wind of
his big steps. Beside him skipped and ran, to
keep step with him, a little man in ill-fitting black,
of whose appearance, thus viewed from the rear,
one could only observe stooping shoulders and
iron-gray hair that curled at the ends.

"He must be the poor missionary who built
his church himself," Mrs. Lossing observed ; "he
is not much of a preacher, the dean said, but he
is a great worker and a good pastor."

Beside him skipped a little man in ill-fitting black.

"So much the better for his people, and the worse for us!" says Harry, cheerfully.

"Why?"

"Naturally. We shall get the poor sermon and they will get the good pastoring!"

Then Harry caught sight of a woman's frock and a profile that he knew, and thought no more of the preacher, whoever he might be.

But he was in the chancel in plain view, after the procession of choir-boys had taken their seats. He was an elderly man with thin cheeks and a large nose. He had one of those great, orotund voices that occasionally roll out of little men, and he read the service with a misjudged effort to fill the building. The building happened to have peculiarly fine acoustic properties; but the unfortunate man roared like him of Bashan. There was nothing of the customary ecclesiastical dignity and monotony about his articulation; indeed, it grew plain and plainer to Harry that he must have "come over" from some franker and more emotional denomination. It seemed quite out of keeping with his homely manner and crumpled surplice that this particular reader should intone. Intone, nevertheless, he did; and as badly as mortal man well could! It was not

so much that his voice or his ear went wrong;
he would have had a musical voice of the heavy
sort, had he not bellowed; neither did his ear
betray him; the trouble seemed to be that he
could not decide when to begin; now he began
too early, and again, with a startled air, he began
too late, as if he had forgotten.

"I hope he will not preach," thought Harry,
who was absorbed in a rapt contemplation of his
sweetheart's back hair. He came back from a
tender revery (by way of a little detour into the
furniture business and the establishment that a
man of his income could afford) to the church and
the preacher and his own sins, to find the strange
clergyman in the pulpit, plainly frightened, and
bawling more loudly than ever under the influence
of fear. He preached a sermon of wearisome
platitudes; making up for lack of thought by
repetition, and shouting himself red in the face
to express earnestness. "Fourth-class Methodist
effort," thought the listener in the Lossing pew,
stroking his fair mustache, "with Episcopal deco-
rations! That man used to be a Methodist minister, and he was brought into the fold by a high-
churchman. Poor fellow, the Methodist church
polity has a place for such fellows as he; but he

is a stray sheep with us. He doesn't half catch
on to the motions; yet I'll warrant he is proud of
that sermon, and his wife thinks it one of the
great efforts of the century." Here Harry took
a short rest from the sermon, to contemplate the
amazing moral phenomenon: how robust can be
a wife's faith in a commonplace husband!

"Now, this man," reflected Harry, growing
interested in his own fancies, "this man never
can have *lived!* He doesn't know what it is to
suffer, he has only vegetated! Doubtless, in a
prosaic way, he loves his wife and children; but
can a fellow who talks like him have any delicate sympathies or any romance about him? He
looks honest; I think he is a right good fellow
and works like a soldier; but to be so stupid as
he is, ought to *hurt !*"

Harry felt a whimsical moving of sympathy
towards the preacher. He wondered why he con-
tinually made gestures with the left arm, never
with his right.

"It gives a one-sided effect to his eloquence,"
said he. But he thought that he understood
when an unguarded movement revealed a rent
which had been a mended place in the surplice.

"Poor fellow," said Harry. He recalled how,

as a boy, he had gone to a fancy-dress ball in
Continental smallclothes, so small that he had
been strictly cautioned by his mother and sisters
not to bow except with the greatest care, lest he
rend his magnificence and reveal that it was too
tight to allow an inch of underclothing. The
stockings, in particular, had been short, and his
sister had providently sewed them on to the
knee-breeches, and to guard against accidents still
further, had pinned as well as sewed, the pins
causing Harry much anguish.

"Poor fellow!" said Harry again, "I wonder
is *he* pinned somewhere? I feel like giving him
a lift; he is so prosy it isn't likely anyone else
will feel moved to help."

Thus it came about that when the dean announced that the alms this day would be given to
the parish of our friend who had just addressed
us; and the plate paused before the Lossing pew,
Harry slipped his hand into his waistcoat pocket
after those two five-dollar notes.

I should explain that Harry being a naturally
left-handed boy, who has laboriously taught himself the use of his right hand, it is a family joke
that he is like the inhabitants of Nineveh, who
could not tell their right hand from their left.

But Harry himself has always maintained that he can tell as well as the next man.

Out drifted the flock of choir-boys singing, " For thee, oh dear, dear country," and presently, following them, out drifted the congregation ; among the crowd the girl that Harry loved, not so quickly that he had not time for a look and a smile (just tinged with rose) ; and because she was so sweet, so good, so altogether adorable, and because she had not only smiled but blushed, and, unobserved, he had touched the fur of her jacket, the young man walked on air.

He did not remember the Saint Bernards until after the early Sunday dinner, and during the after-dinner cigar. He was sitting in the library, before some blazing logs, at peace with all the world. To him, thus, came his mother and announced that the dean and " that man who preached this morning, you know," were waiting in the other room.

" They seem excited," said she, " and talk about your munificence. What *have* you been doing ? "

" Appear to make a great deal of fuss over ten dollars," said Harry, lightly, as he sauntered out of the door.

The dean greeted him with something almost
like confusion in his cordiality; he introduced his
companion as the Rev. Mr. Gilling.

" Mr. Gilling could not feel easy until he
had——"

" Made sure about there being no mistake,"
interrupted Mr. Gilling; " I—the sum was so
great——"

A ghastly suspicion shot like a fever-flush over
Harry's mind. Could it be possible? There were
the two other bills; could he have given one of
them? Given that howling dervish a hundred
dollars? The thought was too awful!

" It was really not enough for you to trouble
yourself," he said; " I dare say you are thanking
the wrong man." He felt he must say something.

To his surprise the dean colored, while the
other clergyman answered, in all simplicity :

" No, sir, no, sir. I know very well. The only
other bill, except dollars, on the plate, the dean
here gave, and the warden remembers that you
put in two notes—I "— he grew quite pale—" I
can't help thinking you maybe intended to put
in only *one !* " His voice broke, he tried to control it. " The sum is so *very* large ! " quavered
he.

" I have given him *both* bills, two hundred
dollars ! " thought Harry. He sat down. He
was accustomed to read men's faces, and plainly
as ever he had read, he could read the signs of
distress and conflict on the prosaic, dull features
before him.

" I *intended* to put in two bills," said he. Gilling gave a little gasp—so little, only a quick ear
could have caught it ; but Harry's ear is quick.
He twisted one leg around the other, a further
sign of deliverance of mind.

" Well, sir, well, Mr. Lossing," he remarked,
clearing his throat, " I cannot express to you
properly the—the appreciation I have of your—
your *princely* gift ! " (Harry changed a groan into
a cough and tried to smile.) " I would like to
ask you, however, *how* you would like it to be
divided. There are a number of worthy causes :
the furnishing of the church, which is in charge
of the Ladies' Aid Society ; they are very hard
workers, the ladies of our church. And there is
the Altar Guild, which has the keeping of the
altar in order. They are mostly young girls,
and they used to wash my things—I mean the
vestments " (blushing)—" but they—they were so
young they were not careful, and my wife thought

she had best wash the—vestments herself, but she
allowed them to laundry the other—ah, things."
There was the same discursiveness in his talk as
in his sermon, Harry thought; and the same
uneasy restlessness of manner. "Then, we give
to—various causes, and—and there is, also, my
own salary——"

"That is what it was intended for," said Harry.
"I hope the two hundred dollars will be of some
use to you, and then, indirectly, it will help your
church."

Harry surprised a queer glance from the dean's
brown eyes; there was both humor and a something else that was solemn enough in it. The
dean had believed that there was a mistake.

"All of it! To *me*!" cried Gilling.

"All of it. To *you*," Harry replied, dryly. He
was conscious of the dean's gaze upon him. "I
had a sudden impulse," said he, "and I gave it;
that is all."

The tears rose to the clergyman's eyes; he
tried to wink them away, then he tried to brush
them away with a quick rub of his fingers, then
he sprang up and walked to the window, his back
to Harry. Directly he was facing the young man
again, and speaking.

"You must excuse me, Mr. Lossing; since my sickness a little thing upsets me."

"Mr. Gilling had diphtheria last spring," the dean struck in, "there was an epidemic of diphtheria in Matin's Junction; Mr. Gilling really saved the place; but his wife and he both contracted the disease, and his wife nearly died."

Harry remembered some story that he had heard at the time—his eyes began to light up as they do when he is moved.

"Why, *you* are the man that made them disinfect their houses," cried he, "and invented a little oven or something to steam mattresses and things. You are the man that nursed them and buried them when the undertaker died. You digged graves with your own hands—I say, I should like to shake hands with you!"

Gilling shook hands, submissively, but looking bewildered.

He cleared his throat. "Would you mind, Mr. Lossing, if I took up your time so far as to tell you what so overcame me?"

"I should be glad——"

"You see, sir, my wife was the daughter of the Episcopal minister—I mean the rector, at the town—well, it wasn't a town, it was two or three

towns off in Shelby County where I had my cir-
cuit.   You may be surprised, sir, to know that I
was once a Methodist minister."

"Invented a little oven or something to steam mattresses and things."

"Is it possible?" said Harry.

"Yes, sir. Her father—my wife's, I mean—
was about as high a churchman as he could be,

and be married. He induced me to join our com-
munion; and very soon after I was married. I
hope, Mr. Lossing, you'll come and see us some
time, and see my wife. She—are you married?"

"I am not so fortunate."

"A good wife cometh from the Lord, sir, *sure!*
I thought I appreciated mine, but I guess I didn't.
She had two things she wanted, and one I did
want myself; but the other—I couldn't seem to
bring my mind to it, no—anyhow! We hadn't
any children but one that died four years ago, a
little baby. Ever since she died my wife has had
a longing to have a stained-glass window, with the
picture, you know, of Christ blessing little children, put into our little church. In Memoriam,
you know. Seems as if, now we've lost the baby,
we think all the more of the church. Maybe she
was a sort of idol to us. Yes, sir, that's one thing
my wife fairly longed for. We've saved our money,
what we *could* save; there are so many calls; during the sickness, last winter, the sick needed so
many things, and it didn't seem right for us to
neglect them just for our baby's window; and—
the money went. The other thing was different.
My wife has got it into her head I have a fine
voice. And she's higher church than I am; so

she has always wanted me to *intone*.   I told her
I'd look like a fool intoning, and there's no mistake about it, I *do !*   But she couldn't see it that
way.   It was 'most the only point wherein we
differed ; and last spring, when she was so sick,
and I didn't know but I'd lose her, it was dread-
ful to me to think how I'd crossed her.   So, Mr.
Lossing, when she got well I promised her, for a
thank-offering, I'd intone.   And I have ever since.
My people know me so well, and we've been
through so much together, that they didn't make
any fuss--though they are not high—fact is, I'm
not high myself.   But they were kind and considerate, and I got on pretty well at home ; but
when I came to rise up in that great edifice, before that cultured and intellectual audience, so
finely dressed, it did seem to me I could *not* do
it !   I was sorely tempted to break my promise.
I was, for a fact."   He drew a long breath.   " I
just had to pray for grace, or I never would have
pulled through.   I had the sermon my wife likes
best with me ; but I know it lacks--it lacks—it
isn't what you need !   I was dreadfully scared and
I felt miserable when I got up to preach it—and
then to think that you were—but it is the Lord's
doing and marvellous in our eyes !   I don't know

what Maggie will say when I tell her we can get
the window. The best she hoped was I'd bring
back enough so the church could pay me eighteen
dollars they owe on my salary. And now—it's
wonderful! Why, Mr. Lossing, I've been thinking so much and wanting so to get that window
for her, that, hearing the dean wanted some car-
pentering done, I thought maybe, as I'm a fair
carpenter—that was my trade once, sir—I'd ask
him to let *me* do the job. I was aware there is
nothing in our rules—I mean our canons—to prevent me, and nobody need know I was the rector
of Matin's Junction, because I would come just in
my overalls. There is a cheap place where I could
lodge, and I could feed myself for almost nothing,
living is so cheap. I was praying about that, too.
Now, your noble generosity will enable me to
donate what they owe on my salary, and get the
window too!"

"Take my advice," said Harry, "donate nothing. Say nothing about this gift ; I will take care
of the warden, and I can answer for the dean."

"Yes," said the dean, "on the whole, Gilling,
you would better say nothing, I think ; Mr. Lossing is more afraid of a reputation for generosity
than of the small-pox."

The older man looked at Harry with glistening
eyes of admiration; with what Christian virtues

"I do believe it was better than the puppies"

of humility he was endowing that embarrassed
young man, it is painful to imagine.

The dean's eyes twinkled above his handkerchief, which hid his mouth, as he rose to make his farewells. He shook hands, warmly. "God bless you, Harry," said he. Gilling, too, wrung Harry's hands; he was seeking some parting word of gratitude, but he could only choke out, "I hope you will get *married* some time, Mr. Lossing, then you'll understand."

"Well," said Harry, as the door closed, and he flung out his arms and his chest in a huge sigh, "I do believe it was better than the puppies!"

13

HARRY LOSSING

THE note-book of Mr. Horatio Armorer, president of our street railways, contained a page of interest to some people in our town, on the occasion of his last visit.

He wrote it while the train creaked over the river, and the porter of his Pullman car was brushing all the dust that had been distributed on the passengers' clothing, into the main aisle.

If you had seen him writing it (with a stubby little pencil that he occasionally brightened with the tip of his tongue), you would not have dreamed him to be more profoundly disturbed than he had been in years. Nor would the page itself have much enlightened you.

> " *See abt road M–D–*
> *See L*
> *See E & M tea-set*
> *See abt L.*"

Translated into long-hand, this reads: "See

about the street-car road, Marston (the superintendent) and Dane (the lawyer). See Lossing,
see Esther and Maggie, and remember about
tea-set. See about Lossing."

His memoranda written, he slipped the book in
his pocket, reflecting cynically, " There's habit !
I've no need of writing that. It's not pleasant
enough to forget !"

Thirty odd years ago, Horatio Armorer—they
called him 'Raish, then—had left the town to
seek his fortune in Chicago. It was his day-
dream to wrestle a hundred thousand dollars out
of the world's tight fists, and return to live in
pomp on Brady Street hill ! He should drive a
buggy with two horses, and his wife should keep
two girls. Long ago, the hundred thousand limit
had been reached and passed, next the million ;
and still he did not return. His father, the Presbyterian minister, left his parish, or, to be exact,
was gently propelled out of his parish by the
disaffected ; the family had a new home ; and the
son, struggling to help them out of his scanty
resources, went to the new parish and not to the
old. He grew rich, he established his brothers
and sisters in prosperity, he erected costly monu-
ments and a memorial church to his parents (they

were beyond any other gifts from him); he married, and lavished his money on three daughters;
but the home of his youth neither saw him nor
his money until Margaret Ellis bought a house on
Brady Street, far up town, where she could have
all the grass that she wanted. Mrs. Ellis was a
widow and rich. Not a millionaire like her
brother, but the possessor of a handsome property.

She was the best-natured woman in the world,
and never guessed how hard her neighbors found
it to forgive her for always calling their town of
thirty thousand souls, "the country." She said
that she had pined for years to live in the
country, and have horses, and a Jersey cow and
chickens, and "a neat pig." All of which modest
cravings she gratified on her little estate; and the
gardener was often seen with a scowl and the
garden hose, keeping the pig neat.

It was later that Mr. Armorer had bought the
street railways, they having had a troublous his-
tory and being for sale cheap. Nobody that
knows Armorer as a business man would back his
sentiment by so much as an old shoe; yet it was
sentiment, and not a good bargain, that had en-
ticed the financier. Once engaged, the instincts

of a shrewd trader prompted him to turn it into a
good bargain, anyhow. His fancy was pleased by

Keeping the pig neat.

a vision of a return to the home of his childhood
and his struggling youth, as a greater personage
than his hopes had ever dared promise.

But, in the event, there was little enough
gratification for his vanity. Not since his wife's
death had he been so harassed and anxious; for
he came not in order to view his new property,
but because his sister had written him her suspicions that Harry Lossing wanted to marry his
youngest daughter.

Armorer arrived in the early dawn. Early as it
was, a handsome victoria, with horses sleeker of
skin and harness heavier and brighter than one is
used to meet outside the great cities, had been in
waiting for twenty minutes; while for that space
of time a pretty girl had paced up and down the
platform. The keenest observer among the
crowd, airing its meek impatience on the platform, did not detect any sign of anxiety in her
behavior. She walked erect, with a step that left
a clean-cut footprint in the dust, as girls are
trained to walk nowadays. Her tailor-made gown
of fine blue serge had not a wrinkle. It was so
simple that only a fashionable woman could guess
anywhere near the awful sum total which that
plain skirt, that short jacket, and that severe
waistcoat had once made on a ruled sheet of
paper. When she turned her face toward the low,
red station-house and the people, it looked gentle,

and the least in the world sad. She had one of
those clear olive skins that easily grow pale;
it was pale to-day. Her black hair was fine as
spun silk; the coil under her hat-brim shone as
she moved. The fine hair, the soft, transparent
skin, and the beautiful marking of her brows were
responsible for an air of fragile daintiness in her
person, just as her almond-shaped, liquid dark
eyes and unsmiling mouth made her look sad. It
was a most attractive face, in all its moods; sometimes it was a beautiful face; yet it did not have
a single perfect feature except the mouth, which
—at least so Harry Lossing told his mother—
might have been stolen from the Venus of Milo.
Even the mouth, some critics called too small for
her nose; but it is as easy to call her nose too
large for her mouth.

The instant she turned her back on the bustle
of the station, all the lines in her face seemed to
waver and the eyes to brighten. Finally, when
the train rolled up to the platform and a young-
looking elderly man swung himself nimbly off the
steps, the color flared up in her cheeks, only to
sink as suddenly; like a candle flame in a gust of
wind.

Mr. Armorer put his two arms and his umbrella

and travelling-bag about the charming shape in
blue, at the same time exclaiming, "You're a
good girl to come out so early, Essie! How's
Aunt Meg?"

"Oh, very well. She would have come too, but
she hasn't come back from training."

"Training?"

"Yes, dear, she has a regular trainer, like John
L. Sullivan, you know. She drives out to the
park with Eliza and me, and walks and runs races,
and does gymnastics. She has lost ten pounds."

Armorer wagged his head with a grin: "I dare
say. I thought so when you began. Meg is
always moaning and groaning because she isn't a
sylph! She will make her cook's life a burden for
about two months and lose ten pounds, and then
she will revel in ice-cream! Last time, she was
raving about Dr. Salisbury and living on beef-
steak sausages, spending a fortune starving
herself."

"She had Dr. Salisbury's pamphlet; but
Cardigan told her it was a long way out; so she
said she hated to have it do no one any good, and
she gave it to Maria, one of the maids, who is
always fretting because she is so thin."

"But the thing was to cure fat people!"

" A Regular Trainer."

"Precisely." Esther laughed a little low laugh, at which her father's eyes shone; "but you see she told Maria to exactly reverse the advice and eat everything that was injurious to stout people, and it would be just right for her."

"I perceive," said Armorer, dryly; "very ingenious and feminine scheme. But who is Cardigan?"

"Shuey Cardigan? He is the trainer. He is a fireman in a furniture shop, now; but he used to be the boxing teacher for some Harvard men; and he was a distinguished pugilist, once. He said to me, modestly, 'I don't suppose you will have seen my name in the *Police Gazette*, miss?' But he really is a very sober, decent man, notwithstanding."

"Your Aunt Meg always was picking up queer birds! Pray, who introduced this decent pugilist?"

Esther was getting into the carriage; her face was turned from him, but he could see the pink deepen in her ear and the oval of her cheek. She answered that it was a friend of theirs, Mr. Lossing. As if the name had struck them both dumb, neither spoke for a few moments. Armorer bit a sigh in two. "Essie," said he, "I guess it is no use to side-track the subject. You know why I came here, don't you?"

"Aunt Meg told me what she wrote to you."

"I knew she would. She had compunctions of conscience letting him hang round you, until she told *me;* and then she had awful gripes because she had told, and had to confess to *you!*"

He continued in a different tone: "Essie, I have missed your mother a long while, and nobody knows how that kind of missing hurts; but it seems to me I never missed her as I do to-day. I need her to advise me about you, Essie. It is like this: I don't want to be a stern parent any more than you want to elope on a rope ladder. We have got to look at this thing together, my dear little girl, and try to —to trust each other."

"Don't you think, papa," said Esther, smiling rather tremulously, "that we would better wait, before we have all these solemn preparations, until we know surely whether Mr. Lossing wants me?"

"Don't you know surely?"

"He has never said anything of—of that— kind."

"Oh, he is in love with you fast enough."

growled Armorer; but a smile of intense relief
brightened his face. " Now, you see, my dear, all
I know about this young man, except that he
wants my daughter—which you will admit is not
likely to prejudice me in his favor—is that he is
mayor of this town and has a furniture store——"

" A manufactory; it is a very large business! "

" All right, manufactory, then; all the same he
is not a brilliant match for my daughter, not such
a husband as your sisters have." Esther's lip
quivered and her color rose again; but she did
not speak. " Still I will say that I think a fellow
who can make his own fortune is better than a
man with twice that fortune made for him. My
dear, if Lossing has the right stuff in him and he
is a real good fellow, I shan't make you go into a
decline by objecting; but you see it is a big shock
to me, and you must let me get used to it, and
let me size the young man up in my own way.
There is another thing, Esther; I am going to
Europe Thursday, that will give me just a day in
Chicago if I go to-morrow, and I wish you would
come with me. Will you mind?"

Either she changed her seat or she started at
the proposal. But how could she say that she
wanted to stay in America with a man who had

not said a formal word of love to her? " I can
get ready, I think, papa," said Esther.

They drove on.   He felt a crawling pain in his
heart, for he loved his daughter Esther as he had
loved no other child of his ; and he knew that he
had hurt her.   Naturally, he grew the more angry
at the impertinent young man who was the cause
of the flitting; for the whole European plan had
been cooked up since the receipt of Mrs. Ellis's
letter.   They were on the very street down which
he used to walk (for it takes the line of the hills)
when he was a poor boy, a struggling, ferociously
ambitious young man.   He looked at the changed
rows of buildings, and other thoughts came
uppermost for a moment.   " It was here father's
church used to stand ; it's gone, now," he said.
" It was a wood church, painted a kind of gray ;
mother had a bonnet the same color, and she used
to say she matched the church.   I bought it with
the very first money I earned.   Part of it came
from weeding, and the weather was warm, and I
can feel the way my back would sting and creak,
now!   I would want to stop, often, but I thought
of mother in church with that bonnet, and I kept
on !   There's the place where Seeds, the grocer
that used to trust us, had his store ; it was his

children had the scarlet fever, and mother went
to nurse them. My! but how dismal it was at
home! We always got more whippings when
mother was away. Your grandfather was a good
man, too honest for this world, and he loved
every one of his seven children; but he brought
us up to fear him and the Lord. We feared him
the most, because the Lord couldn't whip us!
He never whipped us when we did anything, but
waited until next day, that he might not punish
in anger; so we had all the night to anticipate it.
Did I ever tell you of the time he caught me in a
lie? I was lame for a week after it. He never
caught me in another lie."

"I think he was cruel; I can't help it, papa."
cried Esther, with whom this was an old argu-
ment, "still it did good, that time!"

"Oh, no, he wasn't cruel, my dear," said Ar.
morer, with a queer smile that seemed to take
only one-half of his face, not answering the last
words; "he was too sure of his interpretation of
the Scripture, that was all. Why, that man just
slaved to educate us children; he'd have gone to
the stake rejoicing to have made sure that we
should be saved. And of the whole seven only
one is a church member. Is that the road?"

They could see a car swinging past, on a paral-
lel street, its bent pole hitching along the trolley-
wire.

" Pretty scrubby-looking cars," commented Armorer; "but get our new ordinance through the
council, we can save enough to afford some fine
new cars. Has Lossing said anything to you
about the ordinance and our petition to be allowed to leave off the conductors?"

" He hasn't said anything, but I read about it
in the papers. Is it so very important that it
should be passed?"

" Saving money is always important, my dear,"
said Armorer, seriously.

The horses turned again. They were now opposite a fair lawn and a house of wood and stone
built after the old colonial pattern, as modern
architects see it. Esther pointed, saying:

" Aunt Meg's, papa; isn't it pretty?"

" Very handsome, very fine," said the financier,
who knew nothing about architecture, except its
exceeding expense. " Esther, I've a notion; if
that young man of yours has brains and is fond
of you he ought to be able to get my ordinance
through his little eight by ten city council. There
is our chance to see what stuff he is made of!"

"Oh, he has a great deal of influence," said Esther; "he can do it, unless—unless he thinks the ordinance would be bad for the city, you know."

"Confound the modern way of educating girls!" thought Armorer. "Now, it would have been enough for Esther's mother to know that anything was for my interests; it wouldn't have to help all out-doors, too!"

But instead of enlarging on this point, he went into a sketch of the improvements the road could make with the money saved by the change, and was waxing eloquent when a lady of a pleasant and comely face, and a trig though not slender figure, advanced to greet them.

It was after breakfast (and the scene was the neat pig's pen, where Armorer was displaying his ignorance of swine) that he found his first chance to talk with his sister alone. "Oh, first, Sis," said he, "about your birthday, to-day; I telegraphed to Tiffany's for that silver service, you know, that you liked, so you needn't think there's a mistake when it comes."

"Oh, 'Raish, that gorgeous thing! I must kiss you, if Daniel does see me!"

14

"Oh, that's all right," said Armorer, hastily, and began to talk of the pig. Suddenly, without looking up, he dropped into the pig-pen the remark: "I'm very much obliged to you for writing me, Meg."

"I don't know whether to feel more like a virtuous sister or a villanous aunt," sighed Mrs. Ellis; "things seemed to be getting on so rapidly that it didn't seem right, Esther visiting me and all, not to give you a hint; still, I am sure that nothing has been said, and it is horrid for Esther, perfectly *horrid*, discussing her proposals that haven't been proposed!"

" I don't want them ever to be proposed," said Armorer, gloomily.

" I know you always said you didn't want Esther to marry; but I thought if she fell in love with the right man—*we* know that marriage is a very happy estate, sometimes, Horatio!" She sighed again. In her case it was only the memory of happiness, for Colonel Ellis had been dead these twelve years; but his widow mourned him still.

" If you marry the right one, maybe," answered Armorer, grudgingly; " but see here, Meg, Esther is different from the other girls; they got married when Jenny was alive to look after them, and I

knew the men, and they were both big matches,
you know. Then, too, I was so busy making
money while the other girls grew up that I hadn't
time to get real well acquainted with them. I
don't think they ever kissed me, except when
I gave them a check. But Esther and I——"
he drummed with his fingers on the boards, his
thin, keen face wearing a look that would have
amazed his business acquaintances—" you remember when her mother died, Meg? Only
fifteen, and how she took hold of things! And
we have been together ever since, and she makes
me think of her grandmother and her mother
both. She's never had a wish I knew that I
haven't granted—why, d—— it! I've bought my
clothes to please her——"

" That's why you are become so well-dressed,
Horatio ; I wondered how you came to spruce up
so!" interrupted Mrs. Ellis.

" It has been so blamed lonesome whenever she
went to visit you, but yet I wouldn't say a word
because I knew what a good time she had ; but if
I had known that there was a confounded, long-
legged, sniffy young idiot all that while trying to
steal my daughter away from me!" In an access
of wrath at the idea Armorer wrenched off the

picket that he clutched, at which he laughed and
stuck his hands in his pockets.

" Why, Meg, the papers and magazines are always howling that women won't marry," cried he,
with a fresh sense of grievance ; " now, two of my
girls have married, that's enough ; there was no
reason for me to expect any more of them would !
There isn't one d—— bit of need for Esther to
marry ! "

" But if she loves the young fellow and he loves
her, won't you let them be happy?"

" He won't make her happy."

" He is a very good fellow, truly and really,
'Raish. And he comes of a good family——"

· " I don't care for his family ; and as to his being
moral and all that, I know several young fellows
that could skin him alive in a bargain that are
moral as you please. I have been a moral man,
myself. But the trouble with this Lossing (I told
Esther I didn't know anything about him, but I
do), the trouble with him is that he is chock
full of all kinds of principles ! Just as father was.
Don't you remember how he lost parish after
parish because he couldn't smooth over the big
men in them? Lossing is every bit as pig-headed.
I am not going to have my daughter lead the kind

of life my mother did. I want a son-in-law who
ain't going to think himself so much better than I
am, and be rowing me for my way of doing business. If Esther *must* marry I'd like her to marry
a man with a head on him that I can take into
business, and who will be willing to live with the
old man. This Lossing has got his notions of
making a sort of Highland chief affair of the labor
question, and we should get along about as well
as the Kilkenny cats!"

Mrs. Ellis knew more than Esther about Armorer's business methods, having the advantage of
her husband's point of view; and Colonel Ellis
had kept the army standard of honor as well as
the army ignorance of business. To counter-
balance, she knew more than anyone alive what
a good son and brother Horatio had always
been. But she could not restrain a smile at the
picture of the partnership.

"Precisely, you see yourself," said Armorer.
"Meg"—hesitating—"you don't suppose it would
be any use to offer Esther a cool hundred thousand to promise to bounce this young fellow?"

"Horatio, *no!*" cried Mrs. Ellis, tossing her
pretty gray head indignantly; "you'd insult
her!"

" Take it the same way, eh ? Well, perhaps ;
Essie has high-toned notions. That's all right, it
is the thing for women. Mother had them too.
Look here, Meg, I'll tell you, I want to see if this
young fellow has *any* sense ! We have an ordinance that we want passed. If he will get his
council to pass it, that will show he can put his
grand theories into his pockets sometimes ; and I
will give him a show with Esther. If he doesn't
care enough for my girl to oblige her father, even
if he doesn't please a lot of carping roosters that
want the earth for their town and would like a
street railway to be run to accommodate them
and lose money for the stockholders, well, then,
you can't blame me if I don't want him ! Now,
will you do one thing for me, Meg, to help me
out ? I don't want Lossing to persuade Esther
to commit herself ; you know how, when she was
a little mite, if Esther gave her word she kept it.
I want you to promise me you won't let Esther
be alone one second with young Lossing. She is
going to-morrow, but there's your whist-party
to-night ; I suppose he's coming ? And I want
you to promise you won't let him have our ad-
dress. If he treats me square, he won't need to
ask you for it. Well ? "

He buttoned up his coat and folded his arms, waiting.

Mrs. Ellis's sympathy had gone out to the young people as naturally as water runs down hill; for she is of a romantic temperament, though she doesn't dare to be weighed. But she remembered the silver service, the coffee-pot, the tea-pot, the tray for spoons, the creamer, the hot-water kettle, the sugar-bowl, all on a rich salver, splendid, dazzling; what rank ingratitude it would be to oppose her generous brother! Rather sadly she answered, but she did answer: " I'll do that much for you, 'Raish, but I feel we're risking Esther's happiness, and I can only keep the letter of my promise."

" That's all I ask, my dear," said Armorer, taking out a little shabby note-book from his breast-pocket, and scratching out a line. The line effaced read:

" See E & M tea-set."

" The silver service was a good muzzle," he thought. He went away for an interview with the corporation lawyer and the superintendent of the road, leaving Mrs. Ellis in a distraction of conscience that made her the wonder of her ser-

vants that morning, during all the preparations
for the whist-party. She might have felt more
remorseful had she guessed her brother's real plan.
He knew enough of Lossing to be assured that
he would not yield about the ordinance, which he
firmly believed to be a dangerous one for the city.
He expected, he counted on the mayor's refusing
his proffers. He hoped that Esther would feel
the sympathy which women give, without question generally, to the business plans of those near
and dear to them, taking it for granted that the
plans are right because they will advantage those
so near and dear. That was the beautiful and
proper way that Jenny had always reasoned ; why
should Jenny's daughter do otherwise? When
Harry Lossing should oppose her father and re-
fuse to please him and to win her, mustn't any
high-spirited woman feel hurt? Certainly she
must ; and he would take care to whisk her off
to Europe before the young man had a chance to
make his peace! "Yes, sir," says Armorer, to his
only confidant, "you never were a domestic con-
spirator before, Horatio, but you have got it
down fine! You would do for Gaboriau "—
Gaboriau's novels being the only fiction that
ever Armorer read. Nevertheless, his conscience

pricked him almost as sharply as his sister's
pricked her. Consciences are queer things: like
certain crustaceans, they grow shells in spots;
and, proof against moral artillery in one part, they
may be soft as a baby's cheek in another. Armorer's conscience had two sides, business and
domestic; people abused him for a business buc-
caneer, at the same time his private life was pure,
and he was a most tender husband and father.
He had never deceived Esther before in her life.
Once he had ridden all night in a freight-car to
keep a promise that he had made the child. It
hurt him to be hoodwinking her now. But
he was too angry and too frightened to cry
back.

The interview with the lawyer did not take any
long time, but he spent two hours with the superintendent of the road, who pronounced him "a
little nice fellow with no airs about him. Asked
a power of questions about Harry Lossing; guess
there is something in that story about Lossing
going to marry his daughter!"

Marston drove him to Lossing's office and left
him there.

He was on the ground, and Marston lifting the
whip to touch the horse, when he asked: "Say,

before you go—is there any danger in leaving off
the conductors?"

Marston was raised on mules, and he could
not overcome a vehement distrust of electricity.
"Well," said he, " I guess you want the cold
facts. The children are almighty thick down
on Third Street, and children are always trying
to see how near they can come to being killed,
you know, sir; and then, the old women like to
come and stand on the track and ask questions
of the motorneer on the other track, so that
the car coming down has a chance to catch 'em.
The two together keep the conductors on the
jump!"

"Is that so?" said Armorer, musingly; " well,
I guess you'd better close with that insurance man
and get the papers made out before we run the
new way."

"If we ever do run!" muttered the superintendent to himself as he drove away.

Armorer ran his sharp eye over the buildings of
the Lossing Art Furniture Manufacturing Company, from the ugly square brick box that was
the nucleus—the egg, so to speak—from which
the great concern had been hatched, to the handsome new structures with their great arched win-

dows and red mortar. "Pretty property, very pretty property," thought Armorer; "wonder if that story Marston tells is true!" The story was to the effect that a few weeks before his last sickness the older Lossing had taken his son to look at the buildings, and said, "Harry, this will all be yours before long. It is a comfort to me to think that every workman I have is the better, not the worse, off for my owning it; there's no blood or dirt on my money; and I leave it to you to keep it clean and to take care of the men as well as the business."

"Now, wasn't he a d——— fool!" said Armorer, cheerfully, taking out his note-book to mark,

"See abt road M-D-"

And he went in. Harry greeted him with exceeding cordiality and a fine blush. Armorer explained that he had come to speak to him about the proposed street-car ordinances; he (Armorer) always liked to deal with principals and without formality; now, couldn't they come, representing the city and the company, to some satisfactory compromise? Thereupon he plunged into the statistics of the earnings and expenses of the road (with the aid of his note-book), and made the

absolute necessity of retrenchment plain.   Meanwhile, as he talked he studied the attentive
listener before him ; and Harry, on his part, made
quite as good use of his eyes.   Armorer saw a
tall, athletic, fair young man, very carefully,
almost foppishly dressed, with bright, steady blue
eyes and a firm chin, but a smile under his mustache like a child's ; it was so sunny and so quick.
Harry saw a neat little figure in a perfectly fitting
gray check travelling suit, with a rose in the buttonhole of the coat lapel.   Armorer wore no
jewellery except a gold ring on the little finger of
his right hand, from which he had taken the glove
the better to write.   Harry knew that it was his
dead wife's wedding-ring ; and noticed it with a
little moving of the heart.   The face that he saw
was pale but not sickly, delicate and keen.   A
silky brown mustache shot with gray and a Van-
dyke beard hid either the strength or the weakness of mouth and chin.   He looked at Harry
with almond-shaped, pensive dark eyes, so like
the eyes that had shone on Harry's waking and
sleeping dreams for months that the young fellow
felt his heart rise again.   Armorer ended by asking Harry (in his most winning manner) to help
him pull the ordinance out of the fire.   " It would

be," he said, impressively, " a favor he should not forget ! "

"And you must know, Mr. Armorer," said Harry, in a dismal tone at which the president chuckled within, "that there is no man whose favor I would do so much to win ! "

"Well, here's your chance ! " said Armorer.

Harry swung round in his chair, his clinched fists on his knee. He was frowning with eagerness, and his eyes were like blue steel.

" See here, Mr. Armorer," said he, " I am frank with you. I want to please you, because I want to ask you to let me marry your daughter. But I *can't* please you, because I am mayor of this town, and I don't dare to let you dismiss the conductors. I don't *dare*, that's the point. We have had four children killed on this road since electricity was put in."

"We have had forty killed on one street railway I know ; what of it ? Do you want to give up electricity because it kills children ? "

" No, but look here ! the conductors lessen the risk. A lady I know, only yesterday, had a little boy going from the kindergarten home, nice little fellow only five years old——"

" She ought to have sent a nurse with a

child five years old, a baby!" cried Armorer, warmly.

" That lady," answered Harry, quietly, "goes without any servant at all in order to keep her two children at the kindergarten ; and the boy's elder sister was ill at home.   The boy got on the car, and when he got off at the crossing above his house, he started to run across ; the other train-car was coming, the little fellow didn't notice, and ran to cross ; he stumbled and fell right in the path of the coming car ! "

" Where was the conductor ?   He didn't seem much good ! "

" They had left off the conductor on that line."

" Well, did they run over the boy ? Why haven't I been informed of the accident ? "

" There was no accident.   A man on the front platform saw the boy fall, made a flying leap off the moving car, fell, but scrambled up and pulled the boy off the track.   It was sickening ; I thought we were both gone ! "

" Oh, you were the man ? "

" I was the man ; and don't you see, Mr. Armorer, why I feel strongly on the subject ?   If the conductor had been on, there wouldn't have been any occasion for any accident."

" Well, sir, you may be assured that we will take precautions against any such accidents. It is more for our interest than anyone's to guard against them. And I have explained to you the necessity of cutting down our expense list."

" That is just it, you think you have to risk our lives to cut down expenses ; but we get all the risk and none of the benefits. I can't see my way clear to helping you, sir ; I wish I could."

" Then there is nothing more to say, Mr. Lossing," said Armorer, coldly. " I'm sorry a mere sentiment that has no real foundation should stand in the way of our arranging a deal that would be for the advantage of both the city and our road." He rose.

Harry rose also, but lifted his hand to arrest the financier. " Pardon me, there is something else ; I wouldn't mention it, but I hear you are going to leave to-morrow and go abroad with— Miss Armorer. I am conscious I haven't introduced myself very favorably, by refusing you a favor when I want to ask the greatest one possible ; but I hope, sir, you will not think the less of a man because he is not willing to sacrifice the interests of the people who trust him, to please *anyone*. I—I hope you will not object to my asking Miss Armorer to marry me," concluded Harry, very hot and shaky, and forgetting the beginning of his sentences before he came to the end.

"Does my daughter love you, do I understand, Mr. Lossing?"

"I don't know, sir. I wish I did."

"Well, Mr. Lossing," said Armorer, wishing that something in the young man's confusion would not remind him of the awful moment when he asked old Forrester for his Jenny, "I am afraid I can do nothing for you. If you have too nice a conscience to oblige me, I am afraid it will be too nice to let you get on in the world. Good-morning."

"Stop a minute," said Harry; "if it is only my ability to get on in the world that is the trouble, I think——"

"It is your love for my daughter," said Armorer; "if you don't love her enough to give up a sentimental notion for her, to win her, I don't see but you must lose her. I bid you good-morning, sir."

"Not quite yet, sir"—Harry jumped before the door; "you give me the alternative of being what I call dishonorable or losing the woman I love!" He pronounced the last word with a little effort and his lips closed sharply as his teeth shut under them. "Well, I decline the alternative. I shall try to do my duty and get the wife I want, *both*."

"Well, you give me fair warning, don't you?" said Armorer.

Harry held out his hand, saying, "I am sorry that I detained you. I didn't mean to be rude." There was something boyish and simple about the action and the tone, and Armorer laughed. As Harry attended him through the outer office to the door, he complimented the shops.

"Miss Armorer and Mrs. Ellis have promised to give me the pleasure of showing them to them this afternoon," said Harry; "can't I show them and part of our city to you, also? It has changed a good deal since you left it."

The remark threw Armorer off his balance; for a rejected suitor this young man certainly kept an even mind. But he had all the helplessness of the average American with regard to his daughter's amusements. The humor in the situation took him; and it cannot be denied that he began to have a vivid curiosity about Harry. In less time than it takes to read it, his mind had swung round the circle of these various points of view, and he had blandly accepted Harry's invitation. But he

15

mopped a warm and furrowed brow, outside,
and drew a prodigious sigh as he opened the
note-book in his hand and crossed out, "*See L.*"
" That young fellow ain't all conscience," said he,
" not by a long shot."

He found Mrs. Ellis very apologetic about the
Lossing engagement. It was made through the
telephone ; Esther had been anxious to have her
father meet Lossing ; Lossing was to drive them
there, and later show Mr. Armorer the town.

" Mr. Lossing is a very clever young man, very,"
said Armorer, gravely, as he went out to smoke
his cigar after luncheon. He wished he had
stayed, however, when he returned to find that
a visitor had called, and that this visitor was the
mother of the little boy that Harry Lossing had
saved from the car. The two women gave him
the accident in full, and were lavish of harrowing
detail, including the mother's feelings. "So you
see, 'Raish," urged Mrs. Ellis, timidly, " there is
some reason for opposition to the ordinance."

Esther's cheeks were red and her eyes shone,
but she had not spoken. Her father put his arm
around her waist and kissed her hair. " And what
did you say, Essie," he asked, gently, "to all the
criticisms ? "

The old German was complained of everything

A. B. FROST.

"I told her I thought you would find some way to protect the children even if the conductors were taken off; you didn't enjoy the slaughter of children any more than anyone else?"

"I guess we can fix it. Here is your young man."

Harry drove a pair of spirited horses. He drove well, and looked both handsome and happy.

"Did you know that lady—the mother of the boy that wasn't run over—was coming to see my sister?" said Armorer, on the way.

"I did," said Harry, "I sent her; I thought she could explain the reason why I shall have to oppose the bill, better than I."

Armorer made no reply.

At the shops he kept his eye on the young man. Harry seemed to know most of his workmen, and had a nod or a word for all the older men. He stopped several moments to talk with one old German who complained of everything, but looked after Harry with a smile, nodding his head. "That man, Lieders, is our best workman; you can't get any better work in the country," said he. "I want you to see an armoire that he has carved, it is up in our exhibition room."

Armorer said, "You seem to get on very well with your working people, Mr. Lossing."

" I think we generally get on well with them, and they do well themselves, in these Western towns. For one thing, we haven't much organization to fight, and for another thing, the individual workman has a better chance to rise. That man Lieders, whom you saw, is worth a good many thousand dollars ; my father invested his savings for him."

" You are one of the philanthropists, aren't you, Mr. Lossing, who are trying to elevate the laboring classes?"

" Not a bit of it, sir. I shall never try to elevate the laboring classes ; it is too big a contract. But I try as hard as I know how to have every man who has worked for Harry Lossing the better for it. I don't concern myself with any other laboring men."

Just then a murmur of exclamations came from Mrs. Ellis and Esther, whom the superintendent was piloting through the shops. "Oh, no, it is too heavy ; oh, don't do it, Mr. Cardigan !" " Oh, we can see it perfectly well from here ! *Please* don't, you will break yourself somewhere !" Mrs. Ellis shrieked this ; but the shrieks turned to a murmur of admiration as a huge carved sideboard came bobbing and wobbling, like an intoxicated piece of furniture in a haunted house, toward the two gentlewomen. Immediately, a short but powerfully built man, whose red face beamed above his dusty shoulders like a full moon with a mustache, emerged, and waved his hand at the sideboard.

" I could tackle the two of them, begging your pardon, ladies."

" That's Cardigan," explained Harry, " Miss Armorer may have told you about him. Oh, *Shuey !* "

Cardigan approached and was presented. He brought both his heels together and bowed solemnly, bending his head at the same time.

" Pleased to meet you, sir," said Shuey. Then he assumed an attitude of military attention.

" Take us up in the elevator, will you, Shuey?" said Harry. " Step in, Mr. Armorer, please, we will go and see the reproductions of the antique ; we have a room upstairs."

Mr. Armorer stepped in, Shuey following ; and then, before Harry could enter it, the elevator shot upward and—stuck !

" What's the matter?" cried Armorer.

Shuey was tugging at the wire rope. He called, in tones that seemed to come from a panting chest : "Take a pull at it yourself, sir ! Can you move it ? "

Armorer grasped the rope viciously ; Shuey was on the seat pulling from above. " We're stuck, sir, fast ! "

"Can't you get down either ? "

" Divil a bit, saving your presence, sir. Do ye think like the water-works could be busted ? "

"Can't you make somebody hear ? " panted Armorer.

" Well, you see there's a deal of noise of the machinery," said Shuey, scratching his chin with a thoughtful air, " and they expect we've gone up ! "

" Best try, anyhow. This infernal machine may take a notion to drop ! " said Armorer.

" And that's true, too," acquiesced Shuey. Forthwith he did lift up his voice in a loud wailing : " *Oh—h*, Jimmy ! *Oh—h*, Jimmy Ryan ! "

Jimmy might have been in Chicago for any response he made ; though Armorer shouted with Shuey ; and at every pause the whir of the machinery mocked the shouters. Indescribable moans and gurgles, with a continuous malignant

hiss, floated up to them from the rebel steam
below, as from a volcano considering eruption.
"They'll be bound to need the elevator some
time, if they don't need *us*, and that's one comfort!" said Shuey, philosophically.

"Don't you think if we pulled on her we could
get her up to the next floor, by degrees? Now
then!"

Armorer gave a dash and Shuey let out his
muscles in a giant tug. The elevator responded
by an astonishing leap that carried them past
three or four floors!

"Stop her! stop her!" bawled Shuey; but in
spite of Armorer's pulling himself purple in the
face, the elevator did not stop until it bumped
with a crash against the joists of the roof.

"Well, do you suppose we're stuck *here?*"
growled Armorer.

"Well, sir, I'll try. Say, don't be exerting
yourself violent. It strikes me she's for all the
world like the wimmen,—in exthremes, sir, in exthremes! And it wouldn't be noways so pleasant
to go riproaring that gait down cellar! Slow and
easy, sir, let me manage her. Hi! she's working."

In fact, by slow degrees and much puffing,

Mr. Armorer got out, and they left the elevator to its fate.

Shuey got the erratic box to the next floor, where,
disregarding Shuey's protestations that he could
" make her mind," Mr. Armorer got out, and
they left the elevator to its fate. It was a long
way, through many rooms, downstairs. Shuey
would have beguiled the way by describing the
rooms, but Armorer was in a raging hurry and
urged his guide over the ground. Once they
were delayed by a bundle of stuff in front of a
door ; and after Shuey had laboriously rolled the
great roll away, he made a misstep and tumbled
over, rolling it back, to a tittering accompaniment
from the sewing-girls in the room. But he picked
himself up in perfect good temper and kicked the
roll ten yards. " Girls is silly things," said the
philosopher Shuey, " but being born that way it
ain't to be expected otherwise !"

He had the friendly freedom of his class in the
West. He praised Mrs. Ellis's gymnastics, and
urged Armorer to stay over a morning train and
see a " real pretty boxing match" between Mr.
Lossing and himself.

" Oh, he boxes too, does he ?" said Armorer.

" And why on earth would he groan-like?"
wondered Shuey to himself. " He does that, sir,"
he continued aloud ; " didn't Mrs. Ellis ever tell

you about the time at the circus? She was there
herself, with three children she borrowed and an
unreasonable gyurl, with a terrible big screech in
her and no sense. Yes, sir, Mr. Lossing he is
mighty cliver with his hands! There come a yell
of ' Lion loose! lion loose!' at that circus, just
as the folks was all crowding out at the end of it,
and them that had gone into the menagerie tent
came a-tumbling and howling back, and them that
was in the circus tent waiting for the concert
(which never ain't worth waiting for, between you
and me!) was a-scrambling off them seats, making
a noise like thunder; and all fighting and pushing
and bellowing to get out! I was there with my
wife and making for the seats that the fools quit,
so's to get under and crawl out under the canvas,
when I see Mrs. Ellis holding two of the children,
and that fool girl let the other go and I grabbed
it. 'Oh, save the baby! save one, anyhow,' cries
my wife—the woman is a tinder-hearted crechure!
And just then I seen an old lady tumble over on
the benches, with her gray hair stringing out of
her black bonnet. The crowd was *wild*, hitting
and screaming and not caring for anything, and I
see a big jack of a man come plunging down right
spang on that old lady! His foot was right in

the air over her face! Lord, it turned me sick.
I yelled. But that minnit I seen an arm shoot
out and that fellow shot off as slick! it was Mr.
Lossing. He parted that crowd, hitting right and
left, and he got up to us and hauled a child from
Mrs. Ellis and put it on the seats, all the while
shouting : ' Keep your seats! it's all right! it's
all over! stand back!' I turned and floored a
feller that was too pressing, and hollered it was
all right too. And some more people hollered
too. You see, there is just a minnit at such
times when it is a toss up whether folks will quiet
down and begin to laugh, or get scared into wild
beasts and crush and kill each other. And Mr.
Lossing he caught the minnit! The circus folks
came up and the police, and it was all over. *Well,*
just look here, sir ; there's our folks coming out
of the elevator!"

They were just landing ; and Mrs. Ellis wanted
to know where he had gone.

"We run away from ye, shure," said Shuey,
grinning ; and he related the adventure. Armorer fell back with Mrs. Ellis. " Did you stay
with Esther every minute?" said he. Mrs. Ellis
nodded. She opened her lips to speak, then
closed them and walked ahead to Harry Lossing.

Armorer looked—suspicion of a dozen kinds gnawing him and insinuating that the three all seemed agitated—from Harry to Esther, and then to Shuey. But he kept his thoughts to himself and was very agreeable the remainder of the afternoon.

He heard Harry tell Mrs. Ellis that the city council would meet that evening; before, however, Armorer could feel exultant he added, " but may I come late?"

"He is certainly the coolest beggar," Armorer snarled, " but he is sharp as a nigger's razor, confound him!"

Naturally this remark was a confidential one to himself.

He thought it more times than one during the evening, and by consequence played trumps with equal disregard of the laws of the noble game of whist and his partner's feelings. He found a few, a very few, elderly people who remembered his parent, and they will never believe ill of Horatio Armorer, who talked so simply and with so much feeling of old times, and who is going to give a memorial window in the new Presbyterian church. He was beginning to think with some interest of supper, the usual dinner of the family having been sacrificed to the demands of state; then he saw Harry Lossing. The young mayor's blond head was bowing before his sister's black velvet. He caught Armorer's eye and followed him out to the lawn and the shadows and the gay lanterns. He looked animated. Evening dress was becoming to him. "One of my daughters married a prince, but I am hanged if he looked it like this fellow," thought Armorer; "but then he was only an Italian. I suppose the council did not pass the ordinance? your committee reported against it?" he said quite amicably to Harry.

"I wish you could understand how much pain it has given me to oppose you, Mr. Armorer," said Harry, blushing.

"I don't doubt it, under the circumstances, Mr. Lossing." Armorer spoke with suave politeness, but there was a cynical gleam in his eye.

"But Esther understands," says Harry.

"Esther!" repeats Armorer, with an indescribable intonation. "You spoke to her this afternoon? For a man with such high-toned ideas as you carry, I think you took a pretty mean advantage of your guests!"

"You will remember I gave you fair warning, Mr. Armorer."

" Mrs. Ellis was kind enough to put her fingers in her ears and turn her back."

"It was while I was in the elevator, of course. I guessed it was a put-up job; how did you manage it?"

Harry smiled outright; he is one who cannot keep either his dog or his joke tied up. "It was Shuey did it," said he; "he pulled the opposite way from you, and he has tremendous strength; but he says you were a handful for him."

"You seem to have taken the town into your confidence," said Armorer, bitterly, though he had a sneaking inclination to laugh himself; "do you need all your workmen to help you court your girl?"

"I'd take the whole United States into my confidence rather than lose her, sir," answered Harry, steadily.

Armorer turned on his heel abruptly; it was to conceal a smile. "How about my sister? did you propose before her? But I don't suppose a little thing like that would stop you."

"I had to speak; Miss Armorer goes away to-morrow. Mrs. Ellis was kind enough to put her fingers in her ears and turn her back."

"And what did my daughter say?"

"I asked her only to give me the chance to show her how I loved her, and she has, God bless her! I don't pretend I'm worthy of her, Mr. Armorer, but I have lived a decent life, and I'll try hard to live a better one for her trust in me."

" I'm glad there is one thing on which we are agreed," jeered Armorer, "but you are more modest than you were this noon. I think it was considerably like bragging, sending that woman to tell of your heroic feats!"

"Oh, I can brag when it is necessary," said Harry, serenely; "what would the West be but for bragging?"

"And what do you intend to do if I take your girl to Europe?"

" Europe is not very far," said Harry.

Armorer was a quick thinker, but he had never thought more quickly in his life. This young fellow had beaten him. There was no doubt of it. He might have principles, but he declined to let his principles hamper him. There was something about Harry's waving aside defeat so lightly, and so swiftly snatching at every chance to forward his will, that accorded with Armorer's own temperament.

" Tell me, Mr. Armorer," said Harry, suddenly; "in my place wouldn't you have done the same thing?"

Armorer no longer checked his sense of humor. "No, Mr. Lossing," he answered, sedately, "I should have respected the old gentleman's wishes and voted any way he pleased." He held out his hand. "I guess Esther thinks you are the coming young man of the century; and to be honest, I like you a great deal better than I expected to this morning. I'm not cut out for a cruel father, Mr. Lossing; for one thing, I haven't the time for it; for another thing, I can't bear to have my little girl cry. I guess I shall have to go to Europe without Esther. Shall we go in to the ladies now?"

Harry wrung the president's hand, crying that he should never regret his kindness.

"See that Esther never regrets it, that will be better," said Armorer, with a touch of real and deep feeling. Then, as Harry sprang up the steps like a boy, he took out the note-book, and smiling a smile in which many emotions were blended, he ran a black line through

"See abt L."

www.ingramcontent.com/pod-product-compliance
Lightning Source LLC
Chambersburg PA
CBHW030802020726
47499CB00006B/1736